Colonel Cobra: Super Spy

by

Mark Salud

Preface

Back when I was in the beginning of middle school, my father, my brother, my mom and I used to watch a show called "WRESTLING FROM THE OLYMPIC, a show that features pro-wrestling at the Olympic Auditorium in Los Angeles, CA.

During that time the starts included Chavo Guerrero Sr, Raul Mata, Don Muraco, Black Gourmand and Great Goliath, a very young Dino Bravo, and Ernie Ladd.

The first time we saw a live pro-wrestling event might've been in the mid 1970s at the old San Diego Coliseum in Downtown San Diego. We saw Chavo Guerrero in the main event, and some wrestlers like Bob Orton Sr, Mickey Doyle, and Rock Riddle.

A few years later we were able to afford cable television, which opened the door to watching the USA Network and the World Wrestling Federation. So on TV I used to watch Bruno Sammartino, Stan Hansen, Pat Patterson, Bob Backlund, Pedro Morales, and Tito Santana, just to name a few.

For a while we got to view from our cable TV set other territories such as World Class in Dallas with the Von Erichs, Southwest Championship Wrestling with guys like Tully Blanchard and Bob Sweetan, and the Florida area with Dusty Rhodes and Ole Anderson.

We also were able to watch Mid-South Wrestling with Cowboy Bill Watts, seeing wrestlers like Ted Dibiase, Terry Taylor, Buddy Landell, Jake Roberts, and the Junkyard Dog.

Later on we got exposed to the Memphis area, seeing guys like Superstar Bill Dundee, Terry Funk, Joe LeDuc, Stan Lane, Steve Kiern, and of course Jerry The King Lawler.

We would eventually see the AWA when ESPN picked it up. Thus we saw Verne Gagne and his song Greg, Curt Hennig, Larry Zbyszkco, the Road Warriors and Nick Bockwinkle.

Of course when TBS became available, we got to watch WCW, so Ric Flair, Magnum TA, Butch Reed, Arn Anderson, the Midnight Express and the Rock & Roll Express.

My dad still preferred the WWF, now WWE, especially during the times when there was Hulk Hogan, Greg Valentine, Brutus Beefcake, Roddy Piper, Andre the Giant, Paul Orndorff, Bob Orton Jr, Superfly Jimmy Snuka and the Junkyard Dog.

The thing I noticed is that many of the wrestlers first started their careers in the National Football League, like Ernie Ladd, Jim Niedhart, Hacksaw Jim Duggan, Leon White (Vader), and Bill Goldberg.

Anyway, I had this idea of having a guy being a former NFL player and WWE superstar become a secret agent. Thus I came up with the character Kendall Jacobson and the American Secret Intelligence Organization (ASIO).

Chapter One

It's been a month since Kendall Jacobson retired from the pro-wrestling scene. The last time he on in the squared circle, he was a big heel, in a no-disqualification "I Quit" match against the big-time favorite, John Cena.

When Kendall Jacobson was in Kennedy High School, he was quite an athlete. He was a slender 6' 5" , 189 pounds. He was a good-looking, though he never had a girlfriend. Nonetheless, he was a popular guy, and he did academically well.

He played tight end on the school football team, and he was also on the wrestling team.

He would do the same at the University of Saint Claire, where he would really do well He would have limited success in the NFL, spending two years with the Houston Texans before he was finally cut.

He got contacted by a wrestling promoter for World Wrestling Entertainment, and then he made it as the villainous Colonel Cobra. He was promoted as a mercenary leader who delights in inflicting pain to his opponents. His patented finishing maneuver was the flying power-slam, where he picks up his opponent, throws him up in the air and then grabs him to do the power-slam

He had two years of success, three times being the #1 contender for the world championship, losing all three times to the current titleholders and fan favorites. His memorable matches were against Ted Dibiase, Dwayne "The Rock" Johnson, Nature Boy Ric Flair, Edge, and finally, John Cena.

Now, he's in a new kind of training, as a special operations agent for the United States. He gets to keep himself in shape, like he used to do when he was an NFL player and a wrestler. Kendall was doing so great that he exceeded the expectations of those who trained him.

His three trainers were Jim Underwood, Pete Snyder, and Otis Lincoln. The three of them were former United States NAVY SEALS who have been through many missions during their service.

The three of them would bring Kendall to their conference room after he had his workout and shower.

The conference room was well air-conditioned, a large table in the middle and nice comfortable chairs. There was also a large high-definition TV at the end of the room.

"Have a seat, Mr. Jacobson." Otis Lincoln would say. They all sat down. Pete Snyder would turn the big screen on and then he turned on his laptop PC. Up popped the logo of the American Secret Intelligence Organization, ASIO for short.

After a few minutes, came the face of the chief of the ASIO, Fredrick Harrington. His face reminds most people of singer-actor Kris Kristofferson with a tuxedo.

"Gentlemen, good day to you. First of all, I want to congratulate Mr. Kendall Jacobson, who most wrestling fans know as Colonel Cobra. I remember your last match against John Cena. I admit I was rooting against you, but that was in the script, right?"

They all laughed.

"I also did see your TD catch you caught from QB Tony Schaub against the Jacksonville Jaguars. That was your best game, catching 12 passes, one for a touchdown. Too bad your team didn't win many games, but no one really cares about that this time.""

"You had an awesome Collegiate career.", Jim Underwood would say.

Mr/ Harrington would continue. "Anyway, congratulations to you, Mr. Jacobson for completing our intense training to be a member of ASIO. You'll get a chance to be involved in espionage, and of course, you'll be as famous as James Bond, Derek Flint, and Maxwell Smart. And....loving it."

Once again, everyone laughed.

"All kidding aside, gentlemen, Mr. Jacobson, consider yourself a member of the ASIO Team. You've also have displayed excellent qualities as a team leader, like you did when you were on the wrestling team. You had great charisma as a pro wrestler, too, even though at the time I hated your guts."

Laughter again filled the room.

"Anyway, Colonel Cobra, because of your talents, we think you can organize your own team, or if you prefer, you can completely go it alone. However, if you should choose the latter, you will still have agents backing you up."

Kendall would smile and say, "I'm honored to be part of the ASIO, and I'll start off alone and then call for backup. Is that okay?"

"That would be fine, Mr. Jacobson. Do you mind that your code name be 'Colonel Cobra'?"

He'd smile and say, "That's how the wrestling fans used to know me, so that's not a problem."

"We can let Mr. McMahon know you've become a baby-face, if you want." Jim Underwood would say.

"Well, we know that Mr. McMahon is a big heel anyway, Besides, I've kept in touch with Ted Dibiase, The Rock, John Cena and even Stone Cold Steve Austin"

Mr. Harrington would smile and say, "Funny you should mention those gentlemen. I had a chance to contact them Wait just a moment and you'll see their message to you. "

The screen went blue, and then The Rock appears. "Well, well, Colonel Cobra. You've become a secret agent. I wonder what your enemies are thinking. Well, IT DOESN"T MATTER WHAT THEY THINK!!! Cause I know you're going to go a great job kicking their candy asses all over the place. After that,there will be millions, AND MILLIONS of Americans cheering you on. Good luck, Colonel Cobra!!"

The screen turned blue and then there was Ted Dibiase and his familiar maniacal laugh. "Colonel Cobra. I've said many times that everybody has got a price Now you're working for the United States government. Our enemies will pay a heavy price for messing with you." He ended with his maniacal laugh.

The screen turned blue again, and then there was John Cena. "Wow. The last time I faced you was our last pay-per-view event, and I made you say 'I Quit'. Well, that'll be the last time you'll ever say that, because you ain't no quitter. Go Get'em, Cobra." He saluted him and then the screen went blue again.

Finally, there was Stone Cold Steve Austin. "Well, nice going, son. You did enough beating' the hell out of some of your opponents in the field and in the ring. Now ya gonna lay some can of whoop-ass against a bunch of terrorists and other enemies of our country. Colonel Cobra, Super Spy!! Hell, yeah... Anyway, you'll be the best Super Spy in the world, and that's the bottom line, cause Stone Cold said so!!"

After that, Mr. Harrington show on the screen again. "Yeah, Mr. Jacobson. You are definitely on your way up in the ASIO. That is a fact. Now you get to have your own bag of tricks"

Jacobson smiled. "Great, just as long as I don't have a shoe phone or a code of silence."

The others jokingly said in unison, "What??"

Anyway, they opened a small suitcase, and there were an assortment weapons and other devices to use, like a tiny tear gas container, tracking device, projectile, and tiny explosives.

"Dang, I'm going to have fun with these. Heck, when I was a kid I used to play secret agent with my friends. I was always the good guy.' He started to laugh.

"Just a moment, Mr. Jacobson", Mr. Harrington would say. "Apparently, there are two more people who want to wish you the best of luck."

After the screen went blue, Triple H "Hey, Colonel Cobra. Stephanie and I heard about your new job. Nice. Now you get to fight some real bad guys. I can hardly wait to see you in action, bro. Go get 'em"

The screen turned blue again, and lo and behold, there was Vince McMahon. "Ah..... Colonel Cobra, Super Spy. I imagine you'll have a fun time beating up real evil people. Of course I'll forget your last loss to John Cena and remember your victory over The Road Dogg. That was a classic victory. Anyway, your failed attempts to win a championship notwithstanding, you'll be a successful secret agent, and anyone going against you to try to defeat you have NO CHANCE IN HELL!!! Good luck, Colonel Cobra."

Mr. Harrington appeared on the screen again. "All right. We done enough congratulations. It's time to put you to work"

The screen turned into a huge Google Map of the world. After a few beeps on the screen, the focus went to Paris France.

:You'll be taking a trip to Paris, Mr. Jacobson, with all the goodies in this suitcase, and of course, some firepower that you will be getting once you get to Paris. The person you'll be meeting is Jane Dow. This is her picture."

It was a picture of a French woman, obviously. She had long dark hair, in her mid-30s. She looked very attractive.

"Wow," said Jacobson with a surprising look in his face. "I'm impressed. Of course I have to know her first."

"You've got your priorities straight, and I'm impressed." Mr. Harrington would smile as he said that. "Okay, your tickets are right inside your suitcase. Good luck Colonel Cobra."

"Thank you, Mr. Harrington."

With, that, his three trainers would escort him to a private airport.

The plane that Jacobson entered was not exactly like Air Force One, but it's still fancy nonetheless. There were lots of drinks, lots of computers, and video equipment. Jacobson has knowledge of video equipment and computers, so that will be his advantage.

As he sat down, he was greeted by two lovely French twin sisters. "Bon jour, Monsieur Jacobson."

"Oh, yeah. Now I know I'm gonna love being a 'Super Spy'. Good day to you too."

"We are here to make sure you enjoy your trip to Paris,"

Jacobson smiled as he said, "I'm enjoying this plane already and we haven't left the ground."

"We will see you later, Monsieur Jacobson.", they said.

"Yeah. I'll fasten my seat belt while I enjoy this Coca-Cola."

A few hours after the plane was up in the air, the video screen popped up. It was Mr. Harrington.

"Ah, Colonel Cobra. I see you are enjoying your flight."

Jacobson smiled. "So far, I've enjoyed the view, especially inside the plane, if you know what I mean..."

Mr. Harrington started to laugh. "Oh, I suspect you're talking about the Monet twins. Yes, they are part of the French Secret Intelligence Agency. They plan to help you while you're on this plane ride."

"So far they're doing a great job."

"I'm impressed. But enough chatting. It's time we talk about your assignment.'

The screen turned blue again, and there was a picture of a middle-aged man, with hair only on the sides of his head, and somewhat on the chubby side.

"The man you are looking at is retired Lieutenant Winston Bradford . He served in the United States Marine Corp. He's trained in the latest in weapons technology, which he used when he was in Operation New Dawn, formerly Operation Iraqi Freedom, There were 36,117 U.S. Military Casualties in that war, 4,488 dead and 32.223 according to Gettysburgflag.com's web site.

"Among those casualties were Bradford 's platoon. They were sent on some special mission, but something went wrong and most of Bradford 's platoon were killed or severely injured. Those few that were injured have no recollection of what happened on that mission, while there are others that are reportedly missing in action."

"Hmm,... that's sounds suspicious..."

"Yes, and according to intelligence sources in Paris, he is actually living there in a life of luxury in the French Riviera. He recently got a hold of ten million dollars in gold bullion and five million dollars in diamonds."

"Let me ask you this, chief. Has he made any statements concerning that fateful mission?"

"He only mentioned that what happened was not his fault, yet he's not elaborated why."

"Again, that's suspicious. If it wasn't his fault, why won't he talk about it? Is he hiding something or what?"

"Perhaps you can find out what that is. He normally keeps to himself. Only a few people have been able to see him in person. One of them is his secretary, Margot Tremble, and the other is a Sergeant Fredrick Holmes, another surviving member of his platoon. I could be wrong, but this Holmes might have something on him. Your mission is to find out about this Lieutenant Bradford , and if he's up to no good, stop him."

"You got it, chief." Jacobson sips another bottle of soda.

Chapter Two

Once the plane landed at the airport, Jacobson was escorted by the Monet twins. They'd bring him to the baggage claim area. He grabbed the heavy luggage while the lovely ladies carried the small ones.

With that done, they'd find a limousine driver that had the name "Colonel Cobra" displayed. He would meet with the driver. "Bon jour, Monsieur", said the limo driver.

"A good day to you, sir"

After the Monet twins loaded his other baggage in the trunk, they said, "Au revoir, Monsieur."

"Au revoir."

As the driver drove off with Jacobson in it, he would save, "Welcome to Paris, Monsieur. My name is Claude DuPont. I will be driving you to meet with Madame Jane Dow, your international liaison. She is staying at the French Riviera. We will take you there."

"Merci, Claude", Jacobson would say.

It was a beautiful day in Paris. The drive along the streets were breathtaking to Mr. Jacobson. He couldn't help but stare at the women passing by.

He was in awe of the look of the French Riviera. Even during his time in the National Football League, he never went anyplace exotic as this.

As he looked around, he saw Madame Jane Dow standing by the lobby desk. She was wearing a blue mini-dress with black high heels. As she saw Jacobson, she smiled and gestured with her finger for him to come to the front desk. Naturally, he'd walk towards her.

She'd smile at him and say, "You must be Monsieur Jacobson. You obviously know I am Madame Dow."

"Yes, I do. Please to meet you Madame Dow. Where can we continue this conversation?"

"Follow me, Monsieur."

"Oh, yeah——"

They would meet in a private area. They would look at various pictures of Sgt Holmes, Margot Tremble, and Lieutenant Bradford .

Well, Madame Tremble was middle-aged French woman, short-blonde hair, with a curvy figure. Sgt. Holmes looked a lot like many of those drill instructors seen in the movies, while Lieutenant Bradford looked like Pee Wee Herman on steroids.

"That's Bradford ? No wonder he's a recluse."

"Well, I suppose. Only Madame Tremble and Sgt. Holmes have been seen in public more that Lieutenant Bradford . Many reporters have tried and failed. Our best opportunity to get to know him is to pretend we're journalists interested in creating war game tournaments using his latest computer game, BATTLE PLANS.

"Ah, I've played a little bit of that. I started a month ago and now I've been very good at it.

"Have you gone to the highest level yet?" she asked.

"As a matter of fact, I've got through to the highest level three times already."

"Hmm, Sgt Holmes is going to be jealous of you."

Jacobson laughed and said, "In that case, I'll look forward to it."

"Be careful, Monsieur. That could be dangerous."

"Maybe for him, but it'll be fun for me."

They were well prepared as they had press credentials printed out for them. She will be the reported, and he will be the photographer.

They ended up driving at the French Mansion where Bradford apparently lives. After ringing the doorbell, there was a digital security camera on the doorway which clicked on, fixed on them. A female voice from the intercom was heard. "State you name and your business, please."

"Madame Jane Dow, reporter for the International War Games Magazine, along with my photo assistant, Monsieur Kendall Jacobson."

The digital camera clicked as if it was taking photographs. The door opened very slowly, and out of the door came Madame Tremble "Bon jour, Madame Dow, Monsieur Jacobson. Follow me."

The long hallway had pictures of famous Generals, from George Washington to Colin Powell. There were also scale models of soldiers, and glass shelves full of scale model armored tanks, trucks, and jeeps.

Right in the middle of the room was a large round table of scale model airplanes, from the ones from WWI to the ones used in Operation Desert Storm.

"If you will wait here, Sargent Holmes will be here in a few minutes."

"Merci, Madame"

Already fascinated, Jacobson would take pictures.

"So I guess you are fascinated by all these scale models?"

:Oh, sure. I used to build model kits when I was a kid"

"Fascinating, Monsieur. Absolutely fascinating."

To their surprise, Lieutenant Bradford entered the area. "Welcome to my humble mansion. I hope you enjoy my collection of scale model war machines. These are my prize possessions. My favorites, of course, are the current ones, like the V-22 Osprey and the A-10 Warthog."

"It is a pleasure to meet you, Monsieur Bradford ."

"Madame Dow, I know I don't often get out because I don't know a thing about technology. That's what I've got Sgt. Holmes for."

Again, Jacobson was impressed. He said, "Well, I have to admit I'm impressed with your collections. I used to build model kits like this when I was younger. I've since donated them to a local library."

Bradford smiled. "I'm glad to know someone used to build model kits like I do. Mister Jacobson, you used to be a football player and a pro-wrestler. You lived an interesting life."

"Oh, you're too modest, sir. I mean, a veteran of Operation Iraqi Freedom, you've seen action against real enemies—-"

"Ah, if only I could remember what happened that fateful day we stormed the enemy. I could've had that Saddam Insane———"

All of a sudden, Sgt. Holmes marched into the area and saluted. "SIR!!"

"At ease, Sergeant. This is Madame Jane Dow and Mr. Kendall Jacobson."

"Welcome to the mansion, Ms. Dow... Mr. Jacobson..."

Jacobson would smile. "So, Sgt. Holmes, I understand you are the technology expert.

"Yes, Mr. Jacobson. After the war, I started to work at the research and development department at Trifecta Technologies. The game simulates war conditions and players can customize their players. Some are straight out of boot camp, and others are veterans of the US Marines."

"That is impressive, Monsieur."

"Merci, Madame Dow. Each new recruit goes through boot camp just like in real life, and then once they are ready, they are assigned to the mission."

"Interesting, Sergeant Holmes. Is it man vs computer or can there be multiple players?"

"It's the latter, Mr. Jacobson. Perhaps you'd like to give it a try tomorrow night."

"Tomorrow night, Sergeant?"

"Of course. We've invited a few people from every country to compete in an Operation New Dawn tournament. Some of them are Generals, some are war buffs, and I even invited three people from the AL-queda and Hamas. "

"I beg your pardon, Sergeant Holmes?" exclaimed Madame Dow.

"That's right, Madame Dow. You see, in this game, I don't believe in playing favorites. It'll be fun to see how those terrorists react to all the conditions that randomly come up it the game"

After a pause, the Sergeant had a smirk on his face, and then he said, "Mr. Jacobson, I look forward to see you play the game tomorrow night."

He laughed and then he walked away.

Meanwhile Lieutenant Bradford got out a remote control to turn on his large screen TV. It was a commercial promotion for Trifecta Technologies' new war simulator.

"Trifecta Technologies presents our latest war simulator, Battle Plans. Gamers get to participate in a game of wits and wills against an enemy. Go through boot camp, learn the latest technological weapons, and engage in battle. This game is not for the faint of heart. "

Lieutenant Bradford had a sinister smile on his face. "Mr. Jacobson, I look forward to seeing you tomorrow night. Madame Dow, you may come if you wish."

"Merci, Lieutenant." she answered. "It would be a pleasure."

"Madame Tremble will escort you both out the door. Good day."

With that, Madame Tremble would escort Jacobson and Dow out the door. "I hope you enjoyed the tour. It would indeed be a pleasurable night tomorrow." As she said that, she gave Madame Dow a seductive stare, and winked at Jacobson.

"Looking forward to it", Jacobson would say.

As they walked out, Madame Dow looked quite nervous. "Ooh, I hate it when other women do that to me."

"Really" Tremble was coming on to you? I thought she was coming on to me, with that wink—-"

"Monsieur Jacobson, I am not what you Americans call a 'dyke'. Let us get that straight—-"

"Easy, there. I never said you were. Maybe Tremble is, but you're not." He smiled after that, and then Madame Dow would eventually realized he was trying to humor her, so she laughed, and then so did he.

They both would eat dinner at one of the fancy French restaurants.

"Tell me, Monsieur———-"

"Hey, before we go on with this conversation, I want you to call me Kendall. And may I call you Jane?"

"But of course, Kendall."

"Good. Now what were you going to ask me?"

"How do you expect to do tomorrow against all those guests, including the known terrorist groups?"

"Well, in both the NFL and in pro-wrestling, I happen to be a tough competitor, so that will give me the edge I need."

"Well, I must say, you are very confident."

"That's the way I was when played football, high school, college, and the NFL."

"And as Colonel Cobra, the villainous pro-wrestler."

"Absolutely—"

The two of them smiled as they finished their dinner. They would pay for it

It was getting late, so it was time for them to call it a night. They both arrived at the lobby.

"Well, Jane. It's time we call it a night. We both need the rest."

"You're so right, Kendall. Goodnight." She kissed him on the cheek and then she took the elevator up.

Meanwhile, Jacobson would take a separate elevator car.

Chapter Three

Just like he used to do when he was in college football and the NFL, Jacobson would have a good breakfast and then he goes out jogging.

He had this breakfast, and then he was in his sweats when he came out of to the lobby. He'd run into Jane Dow, who was in a tank top and shorts. "I seem to recall you have this routine of eating a decent breakfast and exercising. Mind if I join you?"

"Not at all. I used to go jogging with my teammates when I used to play. Let's do it."

First they would jog around the hotel buildings, the parking lot, and then around the other buildings. It was rather fun for them.

This jogging bit lasted for 20 minutes, and then they went back to their separate rooms to take showers.

The two of them would meet outside again, riding a chauffeured limousine. They would go to a fancy department store to get some attire to wear for the upcoming tournament at Lieutenant Bradford 's place.

Later they would eat dinner somewhere. They started with the Terrine du Chef, petite compotee d'oognons. From there they had the Jarret de Boeuf a facon du pays haricots verts pornmes vapeur.

"You know, Jane, I'll have to admit I've never had French cuisine before. Heck, I dreamed about eating in fancy restaurants when I was playing pro."

"Well, Kendall, I did tell you that you were in for a real treat. Do you like it?"

"Absolutely. Now what's for dessert??"

"Creme Brulee a la confiture—-"

"Ooh. La la, that sounds magnificen:."

The Creme Brulee came. They enjoyed it very much.

"Heck, if only my NFL teammates could see me now."

Just then, a waiter came in to see Jacobson. "Excuse me Monsieur. You have a telephone call."

"Excuse me, Jane—-"

"But of course, Kendall", she said as she smiled.

He was brought to a special booth. This one has a video link to whoever is calling. All Jacobson had to do was to input his birth-date and thumb print.

The video screen first showed Mr. Harrington. "I see you have been invited to a war games tournament. It could be dangerous, so be careful."

"I am aware of the danger, so that's why I'm physically and mentally prepared."

"Good. Someone else wants to wish you luck.'

The screen turned blue for a moment, and then suddenly there was NFL Commissioner Roger Goodell. "How are you, Mr. Jacobson?"

"Hey, Commissioner Goodell. Good to see you—"

"This is the first time I've seen a former NFL player go to pro-wrestling and then a secret agent. I remember Pat Tillman going from NFL to the armed forces. I'm sorry that he's passed away. I hope nothing happens to you as you serve your country. Good luck to you, Mr. Jacobson."

"Thank you, Commissioner."

He'd walk out and Jane Dow was waiting. "Who was that?"

"Oh, that was the NFL Commissioner wishing me luck. He's not a bad guy for a commissioner."

Jane would smile. "Your American sense of humor is something I'll need to get used to."

Suddenly a scream was heard in the background. It turns out a couple of thugs with guns started shooting, but fortunately the bullet holes went through drinking glasses and tables.

Kendall Jacobson would get up to see what was going on. Jane got worried. "Kendall, be careful—-"

"I can handle this" he said as he got up and looked at the gunmen. One of them spoke French as he pointed the gun at him."

Kendall was not frightened as he smiled. "Jane, can you translate that these two bozos are saying?"

Jane was a little frightened, but then she said, "They want everyone to empty their pockets and give up their jewelry."

"Oh. I see." He turned to the gunmen and asked, "Any of you two dumbos speak English?"

Well, one of them did. "Ah, you are an American/"

"That's right, dope. You boys ought to put those guns down. You'll hurt yourselves."

"Do you think you are funny, American? What are you going to do to stop us?"

Kendall would smile and say, "Really. I guess you've never heard of 'Dirty Harry'. We're not gonna let you get away with this"

"What are you talking about, American? Who's we?"

At this point Jane Dow was reaching for something in her purse. It was a rock aimed at the second French gunman. She hit him right at the middle of his head.

The gunman that was talking to Kendall got distracted, just enough for Kendall Jacobson to do the same STONE COLD STUNNER that Stone Cold Steve Austin does to his opponents.

He got up and then he smiled. "I've always wanted to do the Stone Cold Stunner on someone."

The French police showed up and did the rest. One of them was a Lieutenant Mortimer, a slender-looking policeman.

"My name is Lieutenant Claude Mortimer. We saw everything, Monsieur——-"

"Jacobson, Kendall Jacobson."

Jane Dow would speak. "And I am Madame Dow."

"Lieutenant Mortimer smiled. "Very good, What brings you to Paris, Monsieur?"

"I am a very special guest to participate in a war games tournament.
"

"You mean a guest of Monsieur Bradford ?"
"That is correct. I'm prepared for it."
"Well, good luck, Monsieur."
"Merci, Lieutenant",
An applause came from the back of the Lieutenant. It was from Sgt. Holmes. "Brilliant, Mr. Jacobson. I was wondering if I made the right choice to invite you to the tournament. I was right."
"Well, I'm glad you feel that way."
Sgt. Holmes looked at his watch and said, "Well, you've got 90 minutes before the tournament. See you there." After that he walked away.
Kendall looked at Jane and said, "I have a feeling you've used that rock before."
As she picked up the rock, she smiled and said, "My mother gave this to me as a self-defense weapon. This is the first time I ever had to use it."
They both smiled, paid the check, and then they left.
Since there was 90 minutes to kill, they looked outside, admiring the scenery.
"So, Kendall, what do you think of Paris so far?"
He smiled and said, "Well, it's more fascinating than I ever imagined. When this mission is over, I'd like to tell my former teammates about my experiences."
"Of course, what you need now is a date."
He looked at her and smiled, saying, "Well, I thought that's what you were..."
Obviously she was flattered. "You're making me blush...."
"I am? Wow, I hope you're not too uncomfortable about that——"
"Don't be silly. I am flattered." After she said that, she hugged him.

From there they took pictures of themselves all over Paris. They must've spent at least an hour or so doing that.

Of course, it was time to go to Bradford 's mansion so Kendall could participate in the war games tournament. As they went in, they were led to a large room full of desktop PCs on top of several desks.

Those that were invited to participate included members of the AL-queda groups from Mali, Somalia, and Yemen. There was also some other terrorist groups, like the Hamas, that showed up.

Kendall and Jane would sit down away from them, sitting next to some computer game fans from other countries.

He had a chance to speak with some of those computer geeks. "Well, how you guys doing?"

One of them, a French student, would speak. "We are here to play games."

Jane would speak to that student in French. It was a long conversation, and then she said to him, "Merci, Monsieur".

With that done, she had a worried look as she said to Kendall, "Apparently these young people are here to play against anyone to prove they are the best in computer games. They seem to have a lot of confidence in their abilities"

Kendall smiled, saying, "Well, in that case they're no different from me. You know by now how confident I am."

"But you have the experience. These kids don't have that advantage."

"Maybe, but you got to give them credit for being so confident."

Just then, Sergeant Holmes came to the room. "Gentlemen, welcome to the BATTLE PLANS room. You all get a chance to be drill instructors of your own platoons. You can customize what kind of men are going to be on your platoon. You'll all get 45 minutes to customize and train your platoon to become real fighting men. So are there any questions?"

There was silence in the room.

"Very well. You may begin."

The young fellows were definitely eager to get started, and so was Kendall. Each of the contestants were trying meticulously to put together their own platoon.

The terrorist contestants were doing a lot of shouting as they were putting together their team. Everyone else seemed to be calm, including Kendall.

Once the 45 minutes were up, the terrorists finally shouted "Praise be to Allah!!"

Holmes started to laugh. "Well, I guess you all are anxious to go to war. Great. Here's what's going to happen"

The big screen showed a map, similar to what is shown on each player's LCD display. Holmes would get a large stick he used to point at different areas of the map.

"You've been all assigned fortresses. Some of you are in the east, and some of you are in the west. I put the AL-queda and the Hamas in the east, and Mr. Jacobson, you and your friends are in the west."

As the participants sat down on their chairs, suddenly their feet were shackled to the floors, and then their waists were locked to their chairs like seat belts.

One of the terrorists shouted, "What is the meaning of this?"

Holmes started laughing manically. "Mr. Bah-an, you've always boasted your hatred to the west. Now you'll get to show it off. "

With no where to go, the participants would grab their game controllers. "Okay. You'll note on your game controllers. Along with the cursors and the trackball control, you have a few other buttons. The red button is the machine gun fire button and the blue button fires missiles. The white button signals surrender—though I doubt you will be using that one—and finally, the green button is the anti-missile defense button."

They all looked at their game controllers, and it was exactly how Holmes described them.

Holmes started to laugh. "The object of the game is to eliminate your opponents. Oh, and by the way, you will all feel the bullets and the missile hits, thanks to some modern technology. Once the war starts, you'll know what I mean." He started to smirk while the participants start to get nervous.

"Okay, gentlemen. I am going to start the timer"

Holmes would bring out his stop watch. "In exactly 60 seconds, the war will start. You have that long to decide to press the white button and then the locks on your chairs will be released, allowing you your freedom."

After a sigh, he started the timer and said, "Once the buzzer sounds, the war begins. Good luck, gentlemen." He said that with a smirk.

Suddenly there was some tense silence as they waited for the buzzer to sound. Kendall, however, was as relaxed as an NFL player preparing for a game, despite being shackled.

The buzzer sounded, and then it sounded as if all hell broke loose. It sounded as if a real war was taking place.

On the main screen, Holmes is laughing . The participants, with the exception of Kendall, became tense as they fired their machine guns. The Hamas kept shouting as they fired all their guns, while the AL-queda terrorists fired their missiles.

The French students used their anti-missiles Kendall, being as calm as can be, would alternate between weapons.

It looked as if the terrorists had the upper hand, but suddenly the French students started to pick them off one by one with a mixture of machine gun and missile fire. Kendall was calm and collected as he played the game.

As the game got intense, suddenly there were casualties. In fact, it came on both sides, as real bullets somehow killed some of the participants on both sides.

When the game was over, Kendall and three of the French students were the only survivors. They were released from their shackles.

"Well, Mr. Jacobson", said Holmes with a smile, "I'm impressed. You and your friends killed off the terrorists Good job."

The three French students were so astonished their jaws seem to drop.

"Gentlemen, is there a problem?"

One of the students spoke up, but he needed a translator.

Jane, who had been sitting in the back of the room, had to come and translate for him. "He said that he thought this was only a game. He didn't expect there would be any killing."

"Ah, you think war is really a game? Seriously? In war there are casualties, We soldiers accept that!!"

Jane was shocked. "They are game players, not real soldiers."

Kendall would speak. "Do you expect to market this software? I mean, war games is one thing. But this is a deadly game with actual killing."

"Of course, Mr. Jacobson. Real war has actual killing Now you volunteered to participate, so this is on yourselves."

He started to smirk again, and then he said, "You gentlemen are free to go."

They would leave the place, but they certainly felt uneasy.

One of the French students came up to Kendall. "Why did he let us go, Monsieur?"

"My guess is Holmes thinks we'll feel guilty about what he did. He probably expects us to react in one of two ways. Either he thinks we will drive ourselves insane, or he thinks we might report to the proper authorities. If it's the latter, I may not leave France alive."

Chapter Four

It was very early in the morning. Kendall went through his routine morning routine. He had his breakfast and then he went out jogging.

A few minutes before he went out the door, Jane would join him. Naturally they would jog around the same places they did the first day they jogged.

Once they were done, they took showers in their own rooms, and then they got dressed to go out.

As they came out, they met the same French students who were at the mansion.

"Boujour, Monsieur Jacobson. Are you feeling good today?"

"Oh, I doing all right. I got a chance to get some activity done. Now I feel great"

Jane would smile. "So do I. What about you three?"

"Oh, we are just going to, as you Americans say, hang out at our favorite eatery."

"Sweet", Kendall said with a smile. "I already had my breakfast——"

"Ah, Monsieur, you must at least join us for a cup of coffee or something. Maybe a frappucino——-"

Kendall and Jane looked at each other, and finally agreed. "All right."

They would find a Cafe' Du Coin to sit together for coffee. Naturally they would talk about their experience in Bradford 's mansion.

"I just have a very bad feeling about our experience the other day", said one of the students.

"How so?" asked Kendall.

"I do not like to kill someone for real. It is morally wrong to kill someone like that, when it is only a game."

"Yes, I know what you mean."

Jane would have a conversation with the other French student, speaking in French. He sounded furious as he talked about what happened. The third student had to calm him down.

"Personally I don't like killing anyone. As a former NFL player and former pro-wrestler, I play by the rules"

It was then one of them said, "Wait a minute. Did you wrestle in the WWE?"

"Yes, I did. I was Colonel Cobra, the heel."

"Oh, yes. I remember your last match against John Cena——"

"Yeah, yeah, the 'I Quit' match——"

The French students started to laugh a little. "You weren't playing by the rules when you were in the WWE——"

"Yeah, I know. I was the heel. People cheered when I fell victim to Stone Cold Steve Austin's 'stone cold stunner' a few years ago———-"

After Jane started to laugh, she would speak to one of the students in French. After their long conversation, she turned to Kendall, saying, "I told him you used to play American football."

"Oh, yeah. I had more success in college than in the National Football League. I had one good game against the Jacksonville Jaguars, 12 catches for 150 yards and one touchdown."

"Ah, but you do well in the WWE, and now you are here."

Kendall smiled. "Yes, I am here. I wish my teammates could see me now."

"Teammates, monsieur??"

Jane had to explain it in French, and then she said, "American Football is so much fun to watch"

The students shook their heads in affirmation.

"Well, thank you so much for joining us for a nice conversation and coffee."

"Hey, I'm so glad I could come to France and make some friends"

One of the students replied, "It is our pleasure. We must go now, so I guess, as you Americans say, 'Take it easy, dude'——"

"You guys take it easy, too"

The students would go to their car, and as the ignition started, the car disintegrated in a ball of flames. It was obvious that somebody installed a bomb in their car.

Kendall and Jane were shocked by what happened. After a pause, Kendall would angrily say, "Okay. This is more than just an assignment. It's personal!!"

The fire department and police department arrived a few minutes later. While the firefighters put out the fire, the French police would question Kendall and Jane.

The French police officer was an Inspector Andre Dubious, a middle-aged man who was as tall as Kendall. He would speak to Jane first, obviously in French..

After Jane was finished, she turned to Kendall. "This is Inspector Andre Dubious. I told him everything, and he just wants you to confirm want I told him."

"All right."

The Inspector smiled at Kendall. "Monsieur Jacobson, is everything that Madame Dow told me is true? She told me about how you met at the mansion of a Lieutenant Bradford . Is this all true?"

"Yes, it is, Inspector."

"Very well. I appreciate your co-operation. However, you Americans would say, 'Don;t leave town yet'"—

"I have no intention to leave until I get to the bottom of this.. I have an assignment to finish and I intend to finish it."

"Are you investigating this Lieutenant Bradford ?"

"Yes. I'm sure Madame Dow has given you all the details."

"Oui, Monsieur Again, thank you for your co-operation."

After that, Kendall and Jane would look at each other. Jane would then say, "Somehow I have the distinct feeling that either Bradford or Holmes did this and we will be the next targets."

"I'm thinking the same thing."

Just as they were about to walk away, a swarm of French reporters came to the scene. They surrounded Inspector Dubious, who judging by his demeanor was not fond of dealing with reporters.

"I don't envy him one bit", Jane would say as she looked at how the French press inquired about the incident.

"Maybe you don't, but I remember when reporters were on my case when I was in the NFL. I hated it when they ask me why I can't do what I used to do in college. It sucks to be on a losing NFL team."

Suddenly four mysterious figures wearing dark glasses and long overcoats held them at gunpoint.

One of them said, "Did you say a 'losing NFL team', Monsieur?"

Raising his hands, Kendall would say, "What is this?"

Jane had her hands up, and she responded, "I think we are being kidnapped."

One of the gunmen smiled and replied, "You are so right, Madame. You know a lot about Sergeant Holmes and Lieutenant Bradford , so now it's time we take you in."

"Take us in?" asked Jane.

"Madame, do not cause any trouble. Who knows? We may even let you live."

As that gunman spoke those words, Kendall would pull out an old trick from his pro-wrestling days when he pulled out a foreign object to win some of his matches. It was a bag of iron pellets, and he managed to use it to knock the guns off three of their hands.

Meanwhile, Jane took advantage of the situation, using the same rock in her purse to knock out the fourth gunmen.

This would allow Kendall to use his patented maneuver, the flying power-slam, on two of them while Jane kicked the other two in the "inseam".

With that done, she'd say to Kendall, "As you Americans would say, 'Let's beat it.'"

"I'm with you——"

They would make a run for it, taking a unoccupied Renault that still had the keys in them. Jane would drive.

They would drive out of there in a hurry. But they were not out of danger yet.

"Do you see anyone behind us?"

As Kendall looked behind, he stopped dark-blue Mercedes-Benz coming closer. "It looks as if that Mercedes-Benz is is going to follow us. I'm guessing it's those four goons that tried to abduct us."

"Did you know I have seen that American movie 'Bullitt' more than once?"

"Oh, yeah. In fact I've been a big fan of Steve McQueen ever since that movie."

As she looked in the rear-view mirror, seeing that Mercedes Benz coming closer, she said, "I guess it's time for me to, as you Americans would say, 'Put the pedal to the metal.'"—-

"Go for it—-"

She did, and the two cars would be speeding all over the streets of France. Eventually, the French police cars would be right behind them.

The chase would last nearly 10 minutes around the streets of Paris, until suddenly a huge truck came straight towards them. Kendall and Jane would manage to escape when they were able to pass it on the right side before it made a sudden turn, blocking the Mercedes-Benz. This allowed the French police to take whoever was in there in custody.

This allowed them to park the car and watch the police take them in.

Jane would sigh, saying, "Well, as you Americans would say, 'We are not out of the woods yet.'".

"You're right, not by a long shot."

That ended up true, for at that very moment another truck came over to block their path. Out of the truck came four armed soldiers.

Naturally, Kendall and Jane slowly came out of the car, hands up.

"Like you said, we're not out of the woods yet", Kendall would say to Jane,

It would have been true, but then all of a sudden they see a familiar face.

"Pete!!" Kendall shouted.

Out of the truck came Pete Snyder. "Hello, Kendall. We thought you were in danger so we put you under surveillance for a while. It's a goo thing we did."

"I'm glad you did, too. And hey, it felt good to do my patented flying power-slam on one of those dudes."

"Come on. Let's go".

They would all hop inside the big truck. Inside the truck was some sophisticated electronic surveillance equipment, monitored by several technicians inside the truck.

"We can pinpoint your location when you go out, so long as you wear your WWE ring."

Kendall looked at his WWE ring. "Good. I hardly take this think off."

Later Jim Underwood and Otis Lincoln came inside.

"Well, I guess I got some backup, just in case."

"That's right." answered Lincoln. "After your French friends got killed, we knew that you were going to eventually need assistance"

"Too bad my French friends were killed. They could've been some help."

"We're sorry about your friends. There wasn't anything we could've done—-"

Kendall started to nod his head. "Yeah, I know. I can't expect you guys to perform miracles—"

"Easy, guys", Pete would intervene, sensing there might be some tension in light of the turn of events. "Right now we need to figure out a plan to stop Bradford and Holmes."

There was a short silent pause in the room, and then Kendall started to smile. "Right, we are in the same boat."

"Good", agreed Underwood. "You're going to have to use all the skills you've learned to survive this. I'm guessing that Holmes and Bradford will do anything to keep their secret."

"I see", replied Jane. "It's what you Americans call a 'no-brainer'".

"Exactly, Madame Dow. That's why you both need to be careful."

"There is one more thing you need to know", Snyder would say. "Those men who were chasing you are in our custody. They told us that Bradford and Holmes plan to move out of Paris and into an isolated area where they can set up their evil plans."

"Did he give any specific details about when and where they are moving?"

Pete Snyder would press a button and then a big screen with a map of the world on it. He'd use a laser pointer as he pointed to the map, saying, "Obviously, we are here in Paris. According to the information we got, they are planning to move the day after tomorrow. The island they plan to move their operations is located somewhere near the southern part of the Philippines"

"Hmmmm", Jane would say as she studied the map. "That means we'll have to follow them and somehow prevent their plans from taking place."

"Right", agreed Kendall. "I have the tracking device ready to use."

"Good, We'll need it"

Chapter Five

Meanwhile, back at the Bradford mansion, Bradford and Holmes were talking in his study.

"Sir, this Jacobson and that Dow woman are a threat.", Holmes would say to Bradford .

"I agree. Our men lost him and he knows about the killing of those French students. We need to make sure that those two do not interfere with our plans."

"Don't forget that the head man of our secret terrorist organization is not going to tolerate failure."

"Don't remind me, Holmes. We've got the day after tomorrow to load up and get this stuff to our new location."

"We've got the necessary vehicles needed to make the move, sir."

"Good. Now our immediate problem is this Jacobson character. He knows too much and it wouldn't surprise me if he does something to stop our move"

"Let him try, sir. He won't be able to stop us."

Just then the computer screen started to flash, "URGENT MESSAGE FROM THE HEADMASTER OF THE TRIFECTA CORPORATION."

After 10 seconds, the face of a mysterious figure appeared on the screen. The face was that of a middle-aged, white-haired man with a khaki shirt and dark green tie. "Gentlemen, this is General Voss, checking up on your operations", the voice spoke with a German accent.

Bradford and Holmes stood in attention and saluted. Voss saluted back, "At ease, men."

"Sir, we plan to move our operations in two days", Bradford would say.

"Herr Colonel, I understand you and Sergeant Holmes have tested the new war game system", said the General.

"Yes, sir. :Members of the Hamas and the AL-queda have been killed by the system.:"

"I see. Who killed them?"

"Three French students and an American—-"

Voss would smile as he said, "Ah you managed to get an American to do the killing. I am pleased. Who is this American?"

Holmes would reply. "His name is Kendall Jacobson. Here's what we know about him. He had a successful career in college football, two years in the National Football League, and he recently retired from the World Wrestling Entertainment organization. He had been put through the rigors of intense training from an American government agency."

"Ah. He's a football player turned pro-wrestler turned spy. He would be an interesting person to deal with."

Bradford started to look nervous as he asked "Sir, is it really wise for us to challenge this Jacobson fellow?"

Voss would start to smirk. "Herr Colonel, I hope you didn't lose confidence in your own men. You know that he knows too much."

"Very well, General. We'll be ready for him"

After they saluted, General Voss would salute back. "Carry on", he finally said before the screen went blue.

"Make sure the men have all the equipment secured," Bradford ordered to Holmes.

"Yes, sir!"

Back at the ASIO headquarters, Kendall and Jane would prepare themselves to go back out again, unaware of what danger will lie ahead.

"Well, eventually I'll be able to use the gadgets that they gave me. This should be a real challenge."

"You are right", agreed Jane as she drove the Renault. "We'll be in danger the rest of the way, but at least we know there are those who are watching our backs."

"Yeah, that's comforting to know", Kendall said, smiling.

As they drove a few miles near the Bradford mansion, they would see various bobtail trucks parked in front, and a few of Bradford 's men load up electronic equipment in those trucks, such as computers and big screens. "

"Well, obviously they are getting ready to move out", Jane would say.

Right after Bradford 's men went back in the building, Kendall would use the opportunity to put the tracking device behind one of the trucks. With that done, he'd sneak back into the Renault with Jane.

"Might as well get a head start", he said with a smile. After that, he and Jane would leave the area.

Parking far away from the area, they would watch the outside of the mansion at a distance, using binoculars, and then they'd use a listening device in case they pick up any conversations.

It was then they saw Bradford and Holmes come out and look inside the trucks.

"Colonel, we have almost everything loaded. General Voss will be happy that everything is going to go as planned"

"All right, Sergeant Holmes. What else needs to get in the truck?"

"The men are getting the schematics for all the equipment ready. We'll be able to move in two days."

Kendall and Jane were able to get that conversation. "General Voss? He must be the main ringleader", Jane would say.

"Does the ASIO have any information on this General Voss?"

"I believe they do."

Jane would use her Smartphone to contact Pete Snyder. "Monsieur Snyder, Madame Dow. Do you have any information on a General Voss?"

At ASIO headquarters, Pete was on his laptop PC the same time he was on the phone with Jane. He would search ASIO files for General Voss.

Immediately, the screen would come up with a picture of Voss, along with some pertinent information on him. "General Wolfgang Voss, former German mercenary, leader of the TRIFECTA CORPORATION. His company is a game software manufacturer. The last games they developed were football, or soccer to us Americans, basketball, and most recently, a war simulator called BATTLE PLANS. I'm sure you're familiar with that one."

Kendall would shake his head. "Oh, yeah. That's the one we played."

"Well, last year's version obviously didn't include the features you played at Bradford 's mansion. I'm guessing Voss must've paid Bradford and Holmes a lot of money to add more realism to the game."

"That definitely explains everything. Voss must be the one wanting to take over the world, using Bradford and Holmes to do his dirty work."

"It makes sense. Voss has some other use for BATTLE PLANS. Obviously your mission is to find out exactly what those plans are."

"Okay Pete. Jane and I got this."

After the communications ended, they would drive away. They would meet with Pete and Otis back at an abandoned warehouse which would be a temporary ASIO meeting place.

It was time to test all the weaponry that they were supplied with, like a tiny tear gas container, projectile, and tiny explosives.

"Well, now I get to finally use all this stuff", Kendall would say as he laughed a little bit.

"Yes, but just remember these are not toys", Jane would remind him.

"Oh, I know, I have to think when is the best time to use them, like all secret agents do."

"Exactly."

First they examined the projectile, the size of a plastic straw. "This one you can fire anything, and it will reach a maximum distance of 20 miles." Otis would say proudly. "Fortunately, this can be used over and over again."

They tested it with a wad of gum, and then it was aimed at a soda can on top of a table on the other side of the building. It would poke a hole right in the middle of the can.

"Bullseye", Kendall would say with a smile on his face.

The tear gas container had pills the size of ibuprofen tablets, in blue and red. "That one you can throw as far as you can and it'll work", Pete said,

Both Kendall and Jane threw one each across the building. It led out a large amount of gas

"It's a good thing you threw the blue pills, because those are harmless. The red ones are deadly.", Otis would tell them.

"We'll keep that in mind", Kendall said as he shook his head up and down,

Finally there was the tiny explosives, They are approximately the size of golf balls, so they were easy for them to throw. They threw it at a dumpster full of trash located across the other side of the building.

After the loud explosion, that side of the building was cluttered with debris of garbage.

Taking the brooms, Kendall and Jane would walk over there, telling Pete, "It's okay, we got this."

Chapter Six

The next morning, Kendall and Jane would jog around the streets of Paris again, shower, change, and then head on out.

Jane would drive the car around until they reached the Halte Nautique of La Villette, and then as soon as they parked the car, they would rent out a boat.

"Have you ever been on a boat before, Kendall?"

"Well, when I was a young kid. I used to ride one of those cruise boats. We'd get a tour of the harbor and we'd see the sea lions. Passing by the US Navy ships was cool, too. I believe we were in San Diego."

"That must've brought back memories."

"It did, so when I was in the NFL, I remember we were playing the Chargers, and the day before the game I got to go to that harbor cruise that I remember as a kid."

"What was that like?"

"Ah, I got to see the sea lions again, the Maritime Museum, and then we passed by the aircraft carriers. Obviously we couldn't get too close to them, but we did see them."

"That must've been fascinating."

"Oh, yeah. I even got to see inside the USS MIDWAY, the aircraft carrier that was decommissioned and turned into a museum"

"Really?"

"In fact, I got to go back there when the WWE was touring in San Diego. That's where I got to sign autographs and pose for pictures."

"I'm amazed."

"I guess you can say that I had more success in the WWE than the NFL, although I did so some community services during the off-season in Houston."

"Oh, you mean when you played football?"

"Yeah, the two years I was in the NFL. Everyone remembers the game I had against the Jacksonville Jaguars. That was my best NFL game ever. I just wished that coaching staff used me more than they have."

"Do wish you were stilling playing?"

"Oh, sure. My dream was to someday go to the Super Bowl. I'll never get that opportunity."

"Ah, I have seen a few Super Bowls. I had friends who took me to one of those places where they would broadcast American sports. I only understand that the object of the game is to score more 'touchdowns' than the opponents before time runs out."

Kendall would smile as he said to her, "Well, at least you got the idea. I guess you've seen the field goals and extra point tries.."\\

"Oh, you mean when they kick the ball through the goal posts?"

"That's right."

"I understand there is one more way to score."

"Actually two more. For example, when the team scores a touchdown, they have the option of the PAT or the two-point conversion. The other way to score is when the defensive team pushes the offense to their own end zone, That's a 2-point safety."

"What is PAT?"

"Point after touchdown, when the kicker kicks the ball through the goal posts——"

"Oh, I'm beginning to learn more about this American football. The one thing that confuses me is when they stop play because of penalties."

Kendall would smile. "Yeah, that gets to be annoying, especially to the coaches. They get mad when the officials call penalties.'Holding, offense, 10-yard penalty, still second down.'"

As they reached the middle of the river, strange noises could be heard. It got louder. There were three other boats coming behind them, and then one in front of them.

"Oh, brother. We're surrounded."

"Who are they?"

"My guess is they're not a welcoming committee."

As they looked, they noticed that they were all wearing white jackets and white caps. One of them, who was on the boat behind them, had a megaphone, so he used it to speak. "Attention, Mr. Jacobson and Madame Dow. You are completely surrounded."

Jane cleared her throat and said, "Well, you're right. They're not a welcoming committee."

The man with the bullhorn would identify himself. "My name is Van Hess. We are here to capture both of you, orders from the TRIFECTA CORPORATION. You will be our prisoner, so you might as well give yourselves up now!!"

It looks as if Kendall and Jane are in a terrible predicament. However, they remembered their weapons.

"What are you going to do?" Jane asked.

"Just watch", Kendall told her as he put a blue tear gas pill in the projectile.

"Mister Jacobson,, you and Madame Dow need to put your hands up now!! You have five seconds!!"shouted Van Hess.

They would put their hands up all right, Van Hess would put his megaphone down, unaware that Kendall had the projectile in his right hand.

Kendall knew he had to work fast, so he aimed the projectile at the boat where Van Hess was.

BOOM!! The gas surrounds the two boats.

Meanwhile Jane would throw the golf-ball-sized bomb at the boat in front of them. BOOM!!!

This gave them the chance to escape from the boats.

By the time the smoke cleared for Van Hess, they were long gone. "GET THEM!! GET THEM!!"

The two boats would go forward, hoping to catch up to Kendall's boat. The chase would last for 20 minutes.

Suddenly they spot an abandoned ship, so they parked the boat right behind them.

By the time Van Hess' boats saw the abandoned ship from two miles away, they couldn't see Kendall or Jane. "Slow down and be prepared!!" he shouted to his crew.

They would slow down, thinking they could find the American ex-wrestler and his French companion,

There is complete silence for five minutes after they finally reached that ship. His men would get their weapons ready.

"Listen, men" Van Hess would say silently. "They may try to trick us somehow, so be prepared."

They waited, and nothing would happen for another two minutes.

All of a sudden, they hear the sound of a helicopter closing in on them. They'd look up, and they'd stare at it for a few minutes until they realize who was in there.

"SO LONG, SUCKER!!" shouted the man in the helicopter.

Van Hess was confused at what was happening until he saw what looked like golf balls fall from the copter. "NO!!!" he shouted.

It was too late. The golf balls fell on Van Hess' boat, and it exploded.

It turns out that Kendall and Jane were in the copter. "Bullseye!!" Jane shouted.

The pilot of the copter was Pete Snyder. "So much for Van Hess."

With all that, the copter would speed away.

Chapter Seven

Back at the Bradford mansion, there was Sgt. Holmes, Lieutenant Bradford and Madame Tremble were sitting in Bradford 's office.

Holmes would speak first. "Sir, so far every attempt to capture this Jacobson and Dow have failed. We just lost Van Hess and his goons when their boat exploded."

Bradford looked very disturbed. "I know. But we must not give up. We can't let them spoil our plans. We know they know too much, but thus far they have no proof."

Madame Tremble would talk. "Maybe you men should give me a shot. I can succeed where your men have failed. "

Just then, the big screen came on. It was General Voss. They would stand up.

"What is going on? Why have you failed to capture this Jacobson fellow??"

"General", Bradford would answer, "we've sent our teams to get him but apparently they have weapons to counter our attempts"

Voss would be angry. "YOU FOOLS!! You've underestimated this man. Didn't you think the Americans would not equip him with weapons before trying to take down Trifecta Technologies?? You have another 48 hours to get him, show him our plans, and then kill him. Do you understand??"

Madame Tremble spoke up. "General, I think I can be successful."

"You, Madame Tremble?? Just how do you think you can capture this Jacobson??"

"Very simple. American men have a weakness for women in distress."

Suddenly the jaws and Bradford and Holmes dropped and eyes wide open. "What??"

General Voss was also surprised. "Madame Tremble, what are you talking about?"

Tremble would have a smirk on her face. "You forget that I used to be an actress. I'm sure I'll be convincing enough to have those two trust me."

"Really?" exclaimed General Voss, who would pause and then he would smile. "Of course. Never try to do what a woman can do better."

"My thoughts exactly", agreed Tremble

"But let me warn you, Madame Tremble", General Voss would say. "Any failure on your part will be hazardous to your health."

"I understand, Herr General. Rest assured I will not fail."

"I will remember that, Madame Tremble I assure you of that".

The big screen went off.

Holmes looked very skeptical. "Do you really think you can be convincing enough to fool the American?"

"Believe me, Sgt. Holmes. I will succeed."

"I'm not convinced, but best of luck to you anyway."

With that, Madame Tremble would leave the room and out of the mansion.

As she walked out, she gets into her Porsche 914 and drives away. As she drives around the streets of Paris, she spots Kendall and Jane at a coffee shop. She parks her Porsche 914 and goes in.

"Monsieur Jacobson. Madame Dow".

Kendall and Jane would look around until they see Madame Tremble "What do you want?"asked Jane.

"I have come to get away from Lieutenant Bradford and Sgt Holmes. I had no idea that his BATTLE PLANS game would actually kill people—-"

"Really?" exclaimed Kendall. How long have you worked for those two clowns?"

"I would say too long, Monsieur. I wish I never knew those evil men."

"How do we know we can trust you?"

Tremble started to weep. "I might as well tell you. I was forced to work with them when they killed my father. You see, my father was the one who originally came up with the idea of BATTLE PLANS. He wanted to create a war simulator that resembles that of Operation Desert Storm"

"Go on—-"

"My father wanted this to be a training game for soldiers and a just-for-fun games to the regular consumer."

"Really?"

"Oui, Monsieur. My father had met Lieutenant Bradford, who was interested in helping him market the game. They were good friends at first, but a year later Bradford got so greedy, and wanted to explore marketing it to the Hamas and the Taliban. My father wanted no part of it."

Jane would have a puzzled look, and so she and Madame Tremble would converse in French. Kendall would wait patiently until they finished their conversation. He couldn't help but notice that Madame Tremble was weeping.

"Margot——" Jane would say as she tried her best to console Madame Tremble, who started to cry uncontrollably.

"Wow", Kendall would say as he watched her cry. "She's obviously upset about something."

"It is serious" Jane would say as she turned to Kendall. "Her father was tortured by Holmes."

"What does she know about General Voss?"

"My father met General Voss through Sgt. Holmes. Holmes brought my father to Voss, and he threatened physical harm to me if he didn't go along with Voss' vision of creating a game where real people are killed"

"Go on—-"

"Once my father finished creating the project, Holmes forced me to join in. When my father protested, Holmes would slap him around, He even tried to stab Holmes with a knife, but Holmes put a bullet straight to his head———-"

By this time, Tremble started to cry uncontrollably. Jane had to give her a big hug.

Kendall would start pacing around, obviously upset. "You know I knew that there was something I hated about that Holmes. But dammit. That's going way over the line."

Jane could see that Kendall was getting more upset. "Kendall———"

He looked at Jane, put his right hand on his forehead and then waved his left hand. "Say no more, Jane. I know, I need to control myself. I get this image in my head that I do my flying power slam on him, or the DDT, or the Stone-Cold stunner on that asshole"

I understand your anger. I am angry, too. We can't let them get away with this."

"That's right."

After a pause, he turned to Tremble "May I call you Margot??"

"Please do", she answered.

"Margot, I may not be a real experienced spy, but I promise you we will help you get vengeance for your father."

"I do appreciate that, Monsieur Jacobson."

As Madame Tremble went with Jane outside, Kendall would make a phone call. He would speak to Pete Snyder.

"Pete, I need to talk to you about Madame Margot Tremble"

"What about her, Kendall?"

"She came to us claiming she wants no part of Bradford and Holmes. What information do you have on her?"

"Okay. This will take me a few minutes. Stand by."

"Sure."

After a two-minute wait, Pete would have the information. "According to our information, Margot Tremble is the executive secretary of Trifecta. Her father's name is Pierre Tremble, who died under mysterious circumstances."

"Interesting. She told us that her father was tortured and shot in the head by Holmes."

"Well,, we have no knowledge of that. The body was never recovered."

"Oh, great. I don't know if we can completely trust her—-"

"You don't think she's telling the truth?"

"To be honest, Pete, I don't think so."

"Well, don't trust her entirely, but use her to infiltrate the Trifecta organization. She may be leading you into a trap, but then that could be the way to do it."

Kendall would clear his throat. 'Yeah, I think I know what you mean. All right. Thanks, Pete."

Just then, Jane would ask, "Kendall, what's wrong?"

After he looked at Tremble, who was sitting down, he would answer. "I just talked to Pete. According to them, there's no record of her father's death."

"Do you suppose she's leading us to a trap?"

"That"s highly likely. However, we could go ahead and use her to get to the Trifecta Organization and destroy their plans."

"So we must be very careful."

"Absolutely—-"

They would walk to Margot Tremble and then Jane would speak to her in French. Meanwhile, Kendall would wait patiently.

Once she was done talking to her, she turned to Kendall. "I do not completely trust her, but she's our way tin infiltrate their organization. We must beware of a trap."

Kendall shook his head. "Yes, I know. Careful is the optimum word."

With that, they would turn to Madame Tremble "Margot, are Bradford and Holmes going to be moving their stuff sooner or are they on schedule to move in a few days?"

"It will be a few days."

"By now they might know that you have left to find us. I wonder if they know you plan to help us?"

Jane looked very skeptical. "Or set a trap for us——"

Madame Tremble would give Jane a look and say. "You still do not trust me———-"

"No, I do not."

The two women would stare at each other as if they were opponents in a UFC fight. Kendall didn't know what to make of it.

"Look, ladies. I don't know about you two, but I think it's time for us to move on and see if we can find out how we can put a stop to Bradford and Holmes. So what do you say we get ourselves started?"

After a bit of a pause, the two ladies would cease the stare-down and then they agreed. They would leave the coffee shop.

As they were about to go to their vehicle, they heard a strange sound of other vehicles screeching towards them.

"Oh, Sh——-" shouted Kendall as they would take cover. Gun fire would follow.

Jane would check to make sure nothing else would happen. After looking around seeing nothing, she turned to Kendall and said, "As you Americans used to say, the coast is clear."

"Well, apparently Bradford and Holmes must know you've made contact with us. We'd better be on our guard from now on."

Kendall would drive while Madame Tremble would sit in the back seat. A few minutes after they drove away from the coffee shop, Kendall noticed something in his rear view mirror.

"Well, I said we need to be on our guard, and now we've got company."

What he saw was a pair of green Mini-Coopers coming up close. They had to stop as there was a red light in front of them. That's when the little cars got side by side to them.

"Fasten your seat belts. This could be a rough ride."

It would be as Kendall would have to "put the pedal to the metal." Speeds around the streets of Paris reached close to 80 miles per hour.

The chase would last a while until they reached an area where there was road construction. Somehow Kendall was able to maneuver past all the dump trucks and bulldozers. The other cars were not so lucky as one of the bulldozers moved, blocking their path. In fact, the first car wasn't able to stop on time, thus it slammed right into the back of the bulldozer, going up in flames.

As they looked back, they saw they were able to escape so Kendall would drive out of the area.

By this time Madame Tremble was starting to weep uncontrollably. "I wish you could trust me. Those men want to kill me for betraying them—"

"Easy, Margot. Easy", Kendall would say as he kept on driving. We just need to be on our guard. We can't predict what will happen next"

Jane would turn to Madame Tremble The two of them would have a conversation in French. Eventually, Madame Tremble would calm herself down, and the two women hugged each other.

This would make Kendall smile. "Okay. I guess we can be on the same page now."

"Yes, we are", agreed Jane.

Chapter Eight

Word would get out to Holmes and Bradford that the attempt to capture Kendall, Jane, and Margot Tremble failed, as Holmes was on the phone with one of his henchmen.

"What do you mean you couldn't kill or capture them??"

Holmes' face started to turn red as he continued to talk on the phone. "You incompetent fools!! You know that Trifecta does not tolerate failure!! Now you go out there and look for those three. If you fail once again, then Trifecta will send someone to hunt you down. IS THAT CLEAR??!!"

Bradford was a bit more calm. "Stand down, Holmes!!"

As he hung up the phone, Holmes would stand at attention, saying,"SIR......"

"I understand you're upset. Our men have apparently underestimated this Jacobson fellow. What really makes me nervous is that we trusted Margot Tremble to try to fool them."

"Sir, do you think she will try to get back at us?"

Just then, the large screen turned on. It was General Voss. They stood at attention.

"At ease", commanded Voss. "Now what is going on right now?"

"Herr General", answered Bradford, "our men are still following Madame Tremble We just don't know their next move."

"What do you mean you don't know her next move?"

"Sir, Madame Tremble is still working on trying to gain the trust of Jacobson and Dow. We're not sure that she has convinced them."

"You fools!! Didn't you plant any listening device on her before she went?"

"We didn't feel it was necessary because she had been very trustworthy before."

"Really? You realize she could be a liability. She knows a lot about our operations. How do you know she didn't—as you Americans would say—'spill the beans' to Jacobson and Dow?"

There was silence after that question, and that would anger Voss. "This is going to upset our plans to dominate the world."

Holmes would speak. "Sir, we still have our agents getting ready to kidnap the important leaders of the world. All we have to do is to give the signal and all the world leaders will be abducted and land in a secret village in Mindinao, where we plan to set up our main headquarters."

Suddenly General Voss became calm. "I see. Are you sure your men can make it happen?"

Holmes would smile as he replied, "I assure you, Herr General, that plan will take place soon."

"I'm getting a bit skeptical, men, but I'll give your plan a chance. However, any more failures will bring about serious consequences. Is that understood?"

"YES, SIR!!", responded Bradford.

Meanwhile, at Kendall's room, he sat at a round table with Jane and Margot. Apparently Margot had planted a listening device in Bradford's office so they could listen in.

They kept listening in to more conversation, as Holmes would ask Bradford, "All right, sir. What is the next move?? Do we ship out to Mindanao sooner or shall we wait until tomorrow as planned?"

"Hmm Let's give Ms. Tremble the benefit of the doubt. Chances are she may have won their confidence. She knows when we plan to move, so let's stick with it."

"Yes, sir."

At this time Kendall was shaking his head in affirmation, and then he turned to Margot. "Tell me, when did you plant that listening device?"

"I was able to plant it while they weren't looking, just as I was about to leave"

Jane would have a skeptical look, and then she would speak to Margot in French. The conversation lasted three minutes, and then she turned to Kendall. "Well, it seems we have to trust her. My guess is they have sent some of their henchmen to follow us and then capture us."

Kendall seemed to agree. "Well, in that case, we really shouldn't disappoint them. How about we go out, have dinner and go to a casino?"

Jane would smile. "We can do that at the Casino Grand Cercle. There is a restaurant in there and of course, a casino that might rival anything you have in Las Vegas or Atlantic City."

"Oh, yeah? In that case you're on "

Naturally, the three of them would get themselves ready, i.e. shower and change into their best formal wear.

Once they were ready to go, they took a bus to the Casino Grand Cercle. The first thing they would do is dine there.

As they sat down, Jane and Margot would speak to each other in French while Kendall looked at the menu and then looked around the ambiance. "Man, I wish Coach could see me now."

"Pardon?" asked Margot.

Kendall would smile. "I was talking about my NFL coach. I've dreamed about going to places like this but hey, now I am living it up."

Margot would have a confused look. Jane would clarify it for her in French.

"Even in my days in the WWE, I didn't visit places like this. We'd go to most of the well-known eateries in the world. You know, Denny's, Panda Express, McDonalds——"

Margot would start laughing softly. "Monsieur, you amuse me. Yet when I used to see you in the WWE, I hated you."

"Well, that was the job of the heel."

"Heel??"

Once again, Jane would clarify it for her in French. She would smile at him, and then after two minutes of giggling, she turned to Kendall. "You? A bad guy? That's so funny."

"I'll take that as a compliment."

"Oui, Monsieur. It is a compliment."

The three of them would go on to enjoy their meal, and then they would head out to the casino. The most fun they had was at the roulette wheel, as Kendall was winning big.

"Aha. Thirteen black! Should I quit while I'm ahead?"

The two women would laugh. "It's totally up to you."

Kendall would smile, and then he placed his bet. Once again, he won big.

"Yes!" he shouted.

Once again Jane and Margot would smile, and then finally Jane said, "As you Americans say, you are on a roll."

"Ah, you know it, my friend." he replied with a smile.

Just then three men in dark charcoal suits came close to him. "Pardon, Monsieur. We would like to speak with the three of you."

Kendall looked at them suspiciously. "What, for real? I didn't do anything wrong, I hope—-"

"I assure you, this will only take a moment", the one gentleman said as he revealed his gun on his holster. "It is the club rules."

Seeing the weapon, Kendall would sigh and answer, "All right. You've persuaded us."

The three men would lead them to an office. It belongs to a gentleman by the name of Seymour Delawarean, who apparently is the owner of the establishment.

Kendall, Jane and Margot would be allowed to sit on chairs facing Delawarean's desk, while the three dark-suited men stood behind them.

Moments later, Seymour Delawarean would come out. He was a tall and portly fellow with a dark beard and hair that was curled up. He wore a dark blue tuxedo.

"Mister Jacobson", he would say in a deep voice and unmistakably French accent. "My name is Seymour Delawarean, and I own this establishment.

"Really?", Kendall asked. "You almost look like Bray Wyatt."

Delawarean would give him a stoic look for a few seconds, and then he would smile. "I'm very amused with your humor, Mister Jacobson."

"Well, I had a chance to wrestle him. Dude was crazy."

"Do you think I'm crazy, Mister Jacobson?"

"Oh, come on, man. We just met. I can't judge you. "

Jane would speak up, speaking to Delawarean in French. Margot would do likewise.

After their conversation, Delawarean would laugh. "I must say, Mister Jacobson. You have two very loyal friends with you. Now, I really want to speak with you about Trifecta Corporation."

"You want to know something, or do you want to tell me about what you know about them?"

Jane would speak. "Kendall, he is a part of Trifecta."

"Oh, I see. Well, I was on a big winning streak at the roulette table and you guys wanted to stop my streak. I guess you don't want me to break the bank, right?"

Suddenly, Delawarean wasn't amused. "I don't like your attitude, Mister Jacobson. Neither would General Voss—-"

"Oh, I get it. Bradford and Holmes must've sent these goons behind us so you can capture us. Well, let me tell you something, Delawarean. It's free for you to see us, but it'll cost you to lay a hand on us."

"Is that so?" shouted Delawarean.

It would be a real tense situation, and it would get worse as one of the men was ready to throw a switch blade. Fortunately, it missed.

A fight among the six of them was inevitable. Kendall would show off his patented pro-wrestling moves while Jane and Margot made a got showing with some martial arts fighting.

When the dust settled, the three dark-suited men were on the floor, knocked out. Delawarean would pull out his gun. "Mister Jacobson, I am tired of these foolish games"

"Quite frankly, Delawarean, so am I—-"

Before Delawarean could pull the trigger, Kendall was quick as a cricket as he pulled out a red tablet from his pocket, throwing it right at his face.

Since that one had the deadly gas, the reaction to it was inevitable, and the three of them would run out of the casino.

It was a good thing they got out as quick as they did, for just as they ran out, one of the men who they knocked out somehow regained conscience. He was just about to fire his gun at the three of them, unaware that the deadly gas was still filling up the room.

Consequently, before Delawarean could even shout "NO!!" it was too late. The room had exploded.

Naturally there was a panic throughout the place as everyone else ran out in a panic. A few minutes later, the French police would show up, including Lieutenant Mortimer and Inspector Dubois.

After speaking with the others who fortunately escaped, Dubois turned his attention to Kendall and the ladies. "Well, it's obvious that you had what you Americans say a 'close call'."

Kendall would smile. "Oh, yeah. For a moment I thought we were goners—"

Mortimer would turn to the ladies, asking them in French if they were all right. Margot would reply in French that she was all right, and then Jane would follow suit, saying a few more things as well.

"Monsieur Jacobson, I must ask you. Do you plan to.. uh—- Forgive me, but I don't know how to ask this question. Are you planning to-—"

Kendall could see that Mortimer was struggling to ask something. "Lieutenant Mortimer, if you're asking if I plan to hang out a lot longer in Paris, my answer is yes. If you want to know if I plan to follow Lieutenant Bradford and his men to wherever they plan to go, my answer is definitely yes."

"I see. Then perhaps you will require assistance should Bradford's men succeed in capturing the three of you."

"You know, that might be a good idea. Do you have anyone in the French Police willing to watch our backs?"

"It may require the services of the DGSI to do that, Monsieur."

Jane would answer. "That is the Direction générale de la Sécurité Intérieure , or in English, the General Directorate for Internal Security. They are a French security agency, charged with counter-espionage, counter-terrorism, countering cybercrime and surveillance of potentially threatening groups, organizations and social phenomena. "

Kendall would smile. "I'm sure Pete and Otis would be grateful to them for helping us out on this case.

Merci, Lieutenant."

Mortimer would smile. "As you Americans would say, 'don't mention it.'".

Chapter Nine

Back at the mansion, Sergeant Holmes was about to throw a fit, knowing the turn of events at the casino after watching the news.

"Delawarean failed!" shouted Bradford. "This is beginning to be more irritable than ever."

"Sir," Holmes would interrupt, " we still have one more day before we move out to Mindinao. I've checked with the people there and they confirmed that we'll be able to set up shop once we land there."

"I'm still having my reservations regarding Ms Tremble Is she really going to lead them into our trap or is she trying to escape from us??"

"To me, it doesn't matter. Once she returns to us, she's expendable."

Just then the big screen would come on. It was General Voss, so they stood in attention.

"At ease", Voss commanded. "Gentlemen, I'm growing very impatient. This American has caused more trouble than I expected."

"General, we need not change any of the rest of our plans. At this very moment we are carrying out plans to kidnap very important people in the world, including the President of the United States."

"That I will believe when I see it, Bradford. Trifecta doesn't tolerate failure."

The monitor shut off, and then Holmes would continue his rant.

"This is getting really ridiculous!! We have no idea what Tremble is planning. As far as we know, she's turned against us, and that makes her a liability."

Lieutenant Bradford was more upset with Holmes' behavior than what had transpired. "As you were, Sergeant."

Holmes would pause for a moment, and then he turned to Bradford. "Sir, with all due respect, Tremble has not informed us on how she plans to capture Jacobson and Dow. There's too much stalling."

"Sergeant, I understand you're suspicious. Yet somehow I think her plans is to lead them to us, so that when he appears, we won't be surprised and we will have them both where we want them."

"If the Lieutenant is sure, then I will have to respect your beliefs."

"That's better. Even if she does lead them into our trap as we planned, we'll dispose of her anyway."

At this time, Holmes would smile, realizing what Bradford had in mind. "Yes, sir", he replied as he saluted.

With that, they would start packing up, ready to board a plane bound for somewhere in Mindinao.

Just then, Bradford's phone rings. "Bradford——"

After a few minutes, he showed a surprised face. "Well, Ms. Tremble I was worried that you suddenly turned against us."

Holmes, who was also surprised, was nonetheless smiling, thinking that Mr. Tremble didn't betray them after all.

Meanwhile, Bradford listened carefully on the phone. "Yes, I see. Very well, Ms. Tremble We'll be ready for them. Good-day, Ms. Tremble"

Once he hung up the phone, he smiled as if he received good news. "Well, Sargent, we do not have to worry about our female assistant betraying us. She has a plan to lead our Mister Jacobson and Ms. Dow right into our trap."

Did she? Madame Tremble hung up the phone, and as walked about the hotel room that she was staying, she would peek into Jane Dow's room, seeing her asleep. She would have a little smirk on her face.

Suddenly she was startled by a tap on her shoulder. It was Kendall.

"Good morning, Margot. How are you doing?"

"Oh, forgive me, Kendall, you surprised me."

"Really? You know that Jane and I are the only ones here——"

A nervous look on Margot Tremble's face seemed a bit suspicious, but more especially to Jane, who woke up.

Jane looked at her, and the two ladies started to converse in French. Suffice to say that the conversation was a heated one, and then the two of them exchanged slaps in the face.

Kendall didn't know what to do. He could only watch as the two ladies stared at each other like two opponents of an mixed martial arts battle.

After a few minutes, Kendall finally spoke up. "Okay, what's going on?"

Jane was still very upset. "This bitch is leading us right into a trap!!"

He looked at Madame Tremble "For real?!"

As she looked at Jane and Kendall, tears streaming down her cheek, she spoke up. "All right. I just called Lieutenant Bradford and I told him where we are. He should be sending someone over to get us."

Jane was really angry that she slapped her in the face, and Kendall had to restrain her. "Easy, Jane, easy.!"

Once he was able to calm both of them down, he took a look at Madame Tremble. "Okay, Margot. What do you have to say for yourself?"

Madame Tremble would eventually wipe the tears from her eyes and replied, "All right. It's true. I did call Bradford. He's sending his goons over right now."

"Okay, so tell me about your father."

"He was a fool. We were trying to create a war game to rid the world from evil terrorists and superpower governments. My father was totally against war, thinking that's peaceful conference with the United Nations would solve everything."

Kendall began to smile. "At least he was a peaceful man. I like guys like that."

"You don't know what a fool he was. All those terrorists like the Hamas, the Taliban, Somali pirates, know nothing but killing innocent people They deserve to die!!"

"You're so pathetic.. Man, I thought that I met all the people who were so full of hate like Colonel DeBeers. I mean, your father wanted to use peaceful means to deal with terrorism. Why hang around with people like Bradford and Holmes?"

"That's none of your—-"

Before she can finish her sentence, Jane slapped her in the face. The two started fighting. Kendall had to work fast to move away furniture and fragile decorations.

Just as they were about to choke each other, a knock came on the door. Kendall and Jane would draw their guns and hide. "Who is it?"

"Pete Snyder——"

They would put their guns away and let Pete in. He looked around the living room and looked puzzled. "Would someone tell me what's going on?"

Jane would speak. "This woman called Bradford and Holmes."

Pete would look at Madame Tremble "So you're supposed to be Margot Tremble Who are you really?"

There was no time for explanations as they heard some running footsteps. Naturally they would have to hide.

Two mysterious gunmen in blue trench coats walked in, guns in i their hands. One of them said, "Where did they go?"

"Search the place".

As the mysterious gunmen search the place, they don't find anyone. One of them says, "Do you think that Tremble woman sent us on a wild goose chase?"

"I don't know", replied the other guy. "I'm going to contact the Lieutenant."

Using his mobile phone, he would call. "Sir, they must've left before we got here. We checked the room and there's no one in here."

After a pause while listening on his phone, he finally said, "Yes, sir!"

The two of them left the room.

As they drove away from the hotel, we see Pete and Kendall go down the fire escape, while Jane had Madame Tremble handcuffed while they took the elevator.

Taking a van, they were able to drive away, unaware that the two gunman following them witnessed them going.

In the van, Pete would ask his question to Madame Tremble again. "Al right, I ask you again. Who are you really?"

"I am Margot Tremble, but my father is really Lieutenant Bradford."

Kendall and Jane had shocked looks on their face in light of her confession. "Bradford is your father?"

"Oui, Monsieur. Bradford doesn't know it, He had a brief affair with my mother during Operation Iraqi Freedom. She was a reporter for Le Monde"

Jane would answer, "That's a newspaper here in France."

Kendall could only shake his head. "Okay. How did your mother get involved with Bradford??"

Madame Tremble would clear her throat. "She did a story on him, about how he served in Operation Iraqi Freedom. I remember he invited her to dinner to—as you Americans would say—get the scoop on him.

"Anyway, she spent a lot of time with him, and then, apparently they stayed at a hotel where they got very intimate. A few weeks later, she told him that she was pregnant, and he wanted no part of her".

"Okay, so what happened after that?"

"She gave birth to me at one of the hospitals here in France. When I grew up, she never told me who my father was. It was only when she was dying of cancer, she would tell me and prove to me that Bradford is my father."

"So how did you get to work for Bradford?"

"After I went to school, I was able to get a job with Trifecta. I was hired by General Voss."

"Does Voss know you're Bradford's daughter?"

"I told him I was. He didn't believe me at first, but then he really didn't care. He hired me to work with Bradford and Holmes."

Peter looked at bit puzzled. "Well, this puts everything into a new light. How do you feel about Bradford?"

"I have mixed emotions. He's my father, but I despised him for what he did to the old man who originally designed BATTLE PLANS for fun. "

"Now I'm really confused", said Kendall after listening to the story. "Your last name is the same as the inventor of BATTLE PLANS. "

"Pierre Tremble is indeed the inventor of BATTLE PLANS, but he is not my father. He's my grandfather"

"Oh, now that makes a lot of sense. Does Bradford know that?"

"No, As far as he knows he's just another French gamer nerd. Pierre Tremble's real last name is Francois. I don't think Bradford cares. He just wanted BATTLE PLANS for himself, and I helped him."

"Really?"

"After Bradford shot him, he walked away and then I was alone with him. His last words were, 'Margot, I'm your grandfather.'".

At this time Madame Tremble started weeping. Kendall and Jane could only shake their heads, and Pete would do likewise after he said, "Damn!"

For a while there was nothing but silence in the room, until Jane came up with an idea.

"Pete, we need to give her a chance to prove she's on our side. Let her go."

Kendall was a bit confused, but somehow he figured out what Jane was doing. "Pete, she has a point. She knows when Bradford and Holmes plan to move out, and she knows how they plan to move out."

"That's a bit risky, guys, but if you know what you're doing———"

"Rest assured we know exactly what we're doing", Jane would say with a smirk on her face. "Besides, there is a yellow Renault that's been following us since we left the hotel."

She was right. It turns out the two gunmen who saw them escape managed to follow them.

Pete would notice it as well. "Okay, where do we drop her off?"

"Not yet", answered Kendall. "Wait till we cross that bridge."

Sure enough, there was a bridge over a river. They would speed up to the bridge and cross it, while the Renault was suddenly two miles behind, yet to cross the bridge.

The van would stop, and then Jane would drag Madame Tremble out and remove the cuffs. She would grab her by the hair and then she said something to her in French before she returned to the van. They would speed away, leaving Madame Tremble by herself.

Kendall would ask Jane, "I'm curious. What did you say to her?"

Jane would have that smirk on her face as she answered, "I told her if she betrays us, as you Americans would say, I'll kick your ass."

Pete would smile. "I was tempted to do that myself.":

By the time the Renault cross the bridge, Kendall and Jane were long gone. The gunmen would pick up Madame Tremble "What happened?" asked one of the gunmen.

After catching her breath, Madame Tremble would answer. "They found out who I was, and they let me go."

"You're lying!", shouted the other gunmen.

"Do not question my integrity, Monsieur. They plan to follow me as I can lead them to Trifecta and General Voss."

"Ah, so we can set a trap for them and be done with them once and for all." The two gunmen would laugh and Madame Tremble would have a smirk on her face.

Chapter Ten

Pete would drop off Kendall and Jane at a nearby Parisian cafe, and then he said, "Good luck, you guys" before leaving.

"Well, since we are here, we might as well hang out. What do you think?", asked Kendall.

"There are many Parisian cafes, so we might as well hang out. What would you like?"

"Ah, it's close to lunch time, so how about we have lunch?"

"Sandwiches okay?"

"Sure—"

"How do you like your coffee?"

"I can drink it black."

"Then un expresso for two———'

They would laugh, and then they would enter the place.

Meanwhile, from a few yards away, Margot Tremble and the two gunmen are watching them with binoculars. They would converse in French for a while, and then Madame Tremble would say, "it's really important that they are not harmed until they follow us all the way to Mindinao. Is that understood??"

"But, of course, Madame Tremble It would take out all the fun to kill them now."

"That's right".

With that, the three of them drove away.

Meanwhile, Kendall and Jane were enjoying their coffee. It was then Jane would ask him personal questions.

"Forgive me, Kendall, for asking this. Have you ever had a girlfriend?"

Kendall put his coffee down and smile. "Oh, now you want to ask me personal questions".

"Forgive me if you don't want to talk about it———"

"Oh, no. It's all right. I was so concentrated on doing well in high school so that I can play football I didn't make any time to go on dates."

"Ah, but you are a very handsome man———-"

"Thank you.":

"It's just that I would think you would have one relationship."

After a pause, he finally answered, "Well, there was this cheerleader I had been seeing in college. We were friends and she even helped me in one of my math classes."

"What happened to her?"

"She hooked up with the star quarterback, Luke Flores. A few months later, they were killed in an auto accident. He was apparently texting while driving and reports also found he had been drinking as well."

"Drinking and texting while driving. Very dangerous."

":Yes. Doreen was her name. She was a really cute blonde, and her parents were really proud of her for wanting to study biochemistry. I've only met her parents twice, before and after her funeral."

"I see. I only asked because you are a handsome man. I was sexually abused by my mother—-"

"Oh, man. For real?"

"Yes". There was a pause as Jane started to weep. "She had many failed relationships, and when it didn't work out, I would get the physical abuse."

"Ah, man. That sucks. You never knew who your father was?"

"No. Even when I was a child I never met the man. Only my mother's lovers—-"

"So how were you able to get away?"

Luckily the police arrested her and I was put in foster care, with families d'accueil. My foster family was the Dow family, My foster father was an American, Richard Dow, and my foster mother was Claudine LaSalle Dow."

"Were they good to you?"

"Yes", she answered with a smile. Richard Dow is the founder of the ASIO, and they let me join the organization."

"They knew what they were doing when they let you in. You definitely know how to handle yourself."

"Merci—-""

At that very moment, they hugged each other. A small crowd of people witnessed it and began to applaud.

Jane would smile sheepishly, while Kendall would take a bow.

Just then some French music started playing, and the two of them would dance. Naturally the crowd would join in.

To Kendall's surprise, some contemporary American dance music started to play, and the whole place looked like a rave party.

The "party" would last for 80 minutes, and then Pete showed up again. "Hey, let's take you too back to the hotel."

"Okay", agreed Kendall. "I had enough excitement for the night."

They would ride in a white van. Kendall and Jane sat in the back.

"Now tell me, Kendall. Was this party anything like what you have gone to in America?"

After a pause, he answered, "Most of the parties I go to were during the off season. I would hang out with a few of my teammates, and we use to go around dancing with different women. But they liked us, because we treated them nicely, not like some other guys do."

"Interesting. Have you gotten into any fights?"

Kendall would smile, and then he answered. "You know, there was this one time we went to a party after we beat the Raiders, that we got into an altercation. There was this dude who was trying to hit on every woman at the bar. They rejected him, of course, but he wouldn't take no for an answer."

"What kind of man was he?"

"Ah, he was a long-haired fool. He started to get abusive when one of the women stood up to him and demanded he leave. He shouted to her 'Who is gonna make me?' She hit him with a Jack Daniels bottle."

"Over the head?"

"Yeah. Surprisingly he wasn't cut up too bad. He managed to put his throat on her when she tried to run, and that's when I came in and said, 'Hey, stupid, don't you know when you're not wanted?'

"He turned to me and shouted a lot of foul words, and then I said, "Man, you're really good at showing off your stupidity.'"

"Oh, my. And then what happened?"

"He tried to slug me, but I kicked him below the belt, and he cried like a little baby. My teammates got him up and then threw him out of the bar. The crowd went wild and applauded us."

Pete was listening in and he replied, "You gave that guy a free vasectomy".

The three of them laughed as they drove away to return to the hotel.

As they entered the lobby, Pete would say, "You know, pretty soon they'll be another attempt to kill you guys, or if not, maybe Madame Tremble will try to convince you again that she's in danger."

Jane shook her head. "It'll be a cold day in hell before I ever trust that witch."

Kendall would also shake his head. "I don't know, except that she's not what she appears to be."

"That, mon ami, is an understatement."

Pete finally said, "Okay. I get it. I don't trust her anymore than you guys do. The important thing is that we destroy Trifecta."

Just then, they could heard what apparently is a special news broadcast from a large monitor in the lobby. The anchor woman was speaking in French.

"What's going on?", asked Kendall.

Jane, having listened to the message carefully, would translate. "It is really bad. She's saying that a few world leaders and ambassadors have been abducted."

"Oh, No, My guess is Trifecta. "

"Oh, I'll bet my bottom dollar—"

They would listen as the news reported of the abduction of some world leaders and ambassadors. Another monitor had a broadcast from CNN, that extra precautions have been taken to protect the British Prime Minister and the President of the United States.

"Well, at least the Secret Service is on their toes. They get those guys and the world will be in real trouble." Pete would say.

On the French news network, there's video of the French Prime Minister surrounded by bodyguards as well as a sea of reporters.

"Look", said Pete as he turned to Kendall and Jane. "You guys better get some rest. It's no telling what the day will be like tomorrow."

They would agree and then go to their separate rooms.

Chapter Eleven

Kendall's alarm went off, and so per his routine he had his breakfast, and then he went out jogging around the hotel area.

Naturally he finished his jogging in 15 minutes, and then after he took a shower, he got himself dressed up to go.

He was puzzled as he hadn't heard from Jane, so he decided to knock on her room door. There was no answer.

This worried him so he decided to break in and check. "Jane—-"

He would walk in the bedroom and there she was, headphones and sunglasses on, lying on her bed getting a 100% tan.

"OOPS!!" he shouted.

Jane, realizing that Kendall had interrupted her tanning session, took off her sunglasses as well as her headphones and then smiled. "I'm sorry, Kendall. I was just pampering myself."

"Uh, yeah. I can tell. I'll wait in the living room while you do that. I'm a patient guy."

Kendall would sit on the living room couch, waiting. As he waited, he thought about that game against the Jacksonville Jaguars, when he had his best game of that season, 12 catches for 150 yards and one touchdown.

He even remembered when his teammates celebrated with him when he scored. He would sigh as he thought about that memorable game.

Even the memory of his WWE debut as Colonel Cobra, when he faced a jobber named Roger Smith. He manhandled the guy, doing his signature flying body slam. After the three-count, he got up to hear the boos from the crowd as the ring announcer said, "Here's your winner, Colonel Cobra!!"

Suddenly, he was awakened by Jane's voice. "Kendall—-"

As he opened his eyes, he saw Jane wrapped with a pink towel. "Forgive me for keeping you waiting—-"

"Don"t sweat it, Jane. I'm just trying to be a gentleman."

"My dear Kendall, you have already proven that you are a gentleman.":

By this time, Kendall would get up from the couch. "Oh, well, thank you."

As the two of them stared at each other for a few minutes, Jane would smile and then wrap her arms around him after dropping the pink towel.

Kendall was amazed, and he thought to himself, "I wonder if this is how James Bond got started."

This would last for about ten minutes, and then there was a knock at the door. It was Pete Snyder and Jim Underwood.

Being the gentleman, Kendall would say, "Who's there?", and then give Jane back the towel.

"Pete Snyder and Jim Underwood".

Kendall would open the door and let them in. By this time, Jane was able to put on a robe.

"Gentlemen, good to see you. Are there any developments?"

Jim would talk. "Yes, the United Nations just got together for an emergency session regarding the abduction of a few of our world leaders. They are in the UN as we speak."

Pete would add, "We are going to be in contact with the UN as soon as we set up this special communications device."

With that, he would bring out his laptop PC and connected it to a special HDMI box, which would connect to the TV in the hotel. Once the laptop was set up, they showed the video of the special meeting at the UN. The person speaking was a reporter for the UN, Terry Randolph.

"The United Nations Emergency Council convened in a dimly lit chamber deep within the bowels of the UN headquarters. The air was thick with tension, and the flickering fluorescent lights cast eerie shadows on the faces of the assembled diplomats. The world was on the brink of chaos, and the fate of humanity rested on their shoulders.

"The abductions had been swift and precise. One by one, world leaders vanished without a trace. The German Chancellor, the Indian Prime Minister, the Brazilian President—all gone. The Trifecta Corporation, a clandestine organization with tendrils in every corner of the globe, had orchestrated this audacious plot. Their motives remained shrouded in secrecy, but their message was clear: they held the world hostage."

Kendall would shake his head. "Oh, man. This is serious stuff."

Jim would make contact with the assembly there. "Is the British Prime Minister and the President of the United States there?"

"Affirmative", answered Randolph.

The British Prime Minister, Sir William Hawthorne, sat at the head of the table. His steely gaze swept across the room, assessing the remaining leaders. Beside him, President Everrett Reynolds of the United States clenched his fists. They were the last bastions of hope—the only ones who hadn't fallen into the Trifecta's trap.

Jim would continue. "Mr. Prime Minister, Mr. President, we here at the ASIO have a plan to rescue the other world leaders. This is Operation Midnight Diplomacy."

"What is exactly your plan, gentlemen?"asked the Prime Minister.

"Sir, we are sending our best agents, led by Mister Kendall Jacobson and Ms. Jane Dow. Together, they will smack Trifecta. Their leader, General Voss, along with a Lieutenant Winston Bradford and Sargeant Fredrick Holmes, will be brought to justice."

President Reynolds would speak. "Are Jacobson and Dow with you?"

Kendall and Jane would go identify themselves.

"Mr. Jacobson, you look familiar—-"

"Yes, Mr. President. I used to play in the NFL and was a pro-wrestler named Colonel Cobra."

"I must confess I was a big fan of the WWE."

"Thank you, sir."

"Well, I thank the both of you for volunteering in Operation Midnight Diplomacy. It's going to be dangerous, but I understand you two have been trained for dangerous missions."

"Oui, Monseiur President", Jane would say. "As you Americans wouild say, we are up to the task."

"That's right":, agreed Kendall.

The Prime Minister would smile and then he spoke. "Our mission is simple: infiltrate the heart of the Trifecta, rescue our colleagues, and dismantle their network."

The French Foreign Minister, Madame Isabelle Dubois, leaned forward. "But how do we even find them? The Trifecta operates in the shadows."

"We have a lead," President Reynolds said, his voice unwavering. "A cryptic message intercepted from their encrypted channels. 'The key lies in a small island on the Sulu Sea, south of Mindinao, of the Philippines.'"

Pete would pull up the screeen, showing some tiny islands off the Sulu Sea, sound of Mindinao.

SirWilliam stood, pacing. "Our intelligence suggests that the Trifecta's headquarters are hidden beneath the waves, in an underwater cavern beneath that island. We'll assemble a team—a coalition of the willing—to infiltrate their lair."

The Russian Ambassador, Ivan Volkov, raised an eyebrow. "And who will lead this suicide mission?"

Jim would speak. "Mister Ambassador, rest assured that Mr. Kendall and Ms. Dow are ready to tackle this task. We'll also be sending reinforcements from our world counter-espionage team."

The room erupted in debate. The Japanese Prime Minister argued for a joint operation, pooling resources and expertise. The Brazilian Vice President proposed a diversionary attack on the Trifecta's European stronghold. But Sir William silenced them all.

"Gentlemen, this is no time for arguments. It's time for action. Operation Midnight Diplomacy will be carried out. Mr. Jacobson, Ms. Dow, May God be with you."

Kendall and Jane would salute, and Sir William and President Reynolds saluted back.

Once the transmission ended, it was time to go to work. Pete and Jim would supply Kendall and Jane with more weaponry to accomplish the task.

Jane would get another addition to her arsenal. She strapped a microfiber keyboard to her wrist, its keys emitting a soft glow. It was a relic from the past—an artifact from the Commodore Amiga 500 era—but its encryption algorithms were unmatched.

Kendall looked at it in amazement. "Wow, you got yourself another weapon Cool."

Just then, Jane's phne rang. It was Madame Trembley. "What do you want, you pig——"

Her voice was trembling as she answered, "Madame Dow, Bradford and Holmes are moving their equipment now. Their cars are marked as all red Nissan pickup trucks. They are on their way to the Kingman airfied——"

The phone was cut off, but she managed to tell them about the Kingman Airfield. Peter got them map and pointeed the location.

"There it is. It must be the island where they plan to move their equipment

to. It's the smallest, most conspicious one Everything is inside, underwater. "

"That's correct, according to our investigations. A team of mercenaries in Mindinao reported to us that there is indeed an underwater operation there. Apparently they were successful in infiltrating that place. "

Jane would smile. "Well, then we can have them help us get in,"

"That's right. You will be leading them to rescue our kidnapped world leaders and then put Trifecta out of business.:

Kendall would smile and say "and, loving it".

Jane would give Kendall a confused look while the others laughed.

Chapter Twelve

It was off to Kingmen Field for Kendall and Jane. They rode on a huge Humvee, both dressed in combat gear.

Jane would turn to Kendall. "So, are ready to, as you Americans say, rock and roll??"

Kendall smiled and answered, "Heck, Yeah!!!"

It was a rough ride but it turns out that Kingman Field was in the middle of nowhere. Pete would park the Humvee at a long distance near a barb wire fence. "This is as far as I can take you. You'll be on your own—"

Jane would smile and reply, "And.... Loving it—-"

With that they would cut the barb wire fence and make their way to the field. They had to be careful as if they were caught they would be killed.

Most of Bradford's men were wearing dark green T-shirts and khaki pants. They were loading equipment on board a huge vehicle transport plane.

Naturally, they had to get in and then hide out. They noticed another man and another woman packing some heavy artillery. They would sneak up behind them knock them out, bind them and then steal their uniforms.

With that out of the way they would be able to walk among the crowd of people without being noticed.

"Well, this is the first time I've ever had to disguise myself." Kendall would say as they walked past a few of them.

\

"You mean you never dressed up for Halloween?"

"Are you kidding? I was just not into that crazy scene."

"Well, the last time I dressed up for Halloween, I was Elvira, Mistress of the Dark."

"Really? I wished I could've seen that."

"Kendall, you are so funny."

They would laugh, and then someone came to them and said. "Hey, we need someone to drive that truck that connects our whole network together. Move it."

Without hesitation, they would go to that truck and drive in into the large cargo plane. Once all the equipment was loaded, they were ready to go.

Just then they heard a familiar voice. It was Holmes."Everybody, we are so grateful for the contributions you have made to Trifecta. Together, we will make history."

Fortunately Kendall and Jane were way in the back of the crowd so Holmes couldn't see them.

Holmes continued, "In a few minutes, the world leaders will be playing our game, a real war game called BATTLE PLANS. You made that all happen, and for that, General Voss, Lieutenant Bradford and I thank you from the bottom of our hearts."

The crowd would start cheering.

Holmes kept going. "Once those world leaders are done away with, we will be the rulers of this universe. And now, you'll all be going to your new home. In that plane over there."

He was pointing to a 747 passenger jumbo jet. "Let's go".

They would all go single file in the plane, and Kendall and Jane would board while hiding their faces.

The planes took off to their destination, an island on the Sulu Sea south of Mindindao.

Later the movie screen went down. They started showing Warner Brothers cartoons.

"Kendall would smile as he said "Oh, Bugs Bunny and Road Runner. I guess they couldn't afford to put on any blockbuster movies. "

Jane smiled as she said, ":You know, the Road Runner was my favorite character."

"Really? Cool, We have something in common."

The plane ride was smooth sailing, and then a few hours later they were surrounded by white helicopters with the word TRIFECTA written on them.

The captain of the plane would speak. "Attention, passengers. This is your captain speaking. Do not be alarmed by the helicopters surrounding us. It's just a welcoming party. In a few minutes you will need to fasten your seat belts, extinguish all cigarettes, and most of all, relax. You're home."

Kendall and Jane would look at each other and said in unison, "Yeah, Right."

The copters surrounded the plane, two in front and two in the back. It felt as if they were important people being escorted.

Suddenly, something weird appeared on one of the small islands. It looked like a runway, the length of two football fields, coming out of the water.

A few minutes later, there would be a big truck coming out, driving around the big runway as if to suck up any excess water on the surface.

Once the driver finished, he got out his transmitter. "TRIFECTA ONE to White eagle. You're clear to land."

With that, the plane would land on the runway with the copters still leading as escorts.

"Attention, passengers. This is your captain speaking again. Please remain in your seats as Trifecta prepares you for what's ahead. This should take about 15 minutes. Thank you. "

Kendall and Jane would look around. "Well, this is definitely not anything I've seen before."

"Well, you've done a lot more traveling than I have."

"Oui, I have traveled all over. This is obviously a new experience for you."

"No doubt about that. The only thing is, we're just visiting, and we don't want to live here."

A loud beep would be heard, and a voice saying "All personnel please clear the runway."

The runway was clear, and then straight out from the ground came some glass domes. One was coming from the left side while the other came from the right side.

Once the dome was sealed tight, suddenly the entire runway goes down slowly like an elevator.

By the time it reached its destination, it was all dark. However, the lights started to come on and the place where they landed seemed to be long and wide.

Kendall looked, and then he said, 'Dang. Our NFL road trips were nothing like this. It looks like the Astrodome."

"The Astrodome??"

"Yeah, that used to be where the Houston Oilers used to play, and the Houston Astros. "

"Ah, I see. One of these days I would like to go to a football game, or a WWE event. "

"Sure, I'd be glad to take you there."

A few minutes later, Bradford showed up inside the plane. "Ladies and gentlemen, on behalf of General Voss, I wish to welcome you all to TRIFECTA. We'll all meet in the Four Horsemen's Assembly Hall, where General Voss will address you."

Fortunately for Kendall and Jane, Bradford was unaware that they were among the passengers. He would get outside of the plane, and then the flight attendants instructed them to get off the plane.

They would follow a couple of Bradford's henchmen to the Four Horsemen's Assembly Hall. That's when Kendall saw some familiar pictures all over the walls.

"Holy Power Slam!! I know those guys"he said as he saw the pictures.

"You do?" asked Jane.

"Of course. Ric Flair, Ole Anderson, Arn Anderson, Tully Blanchard, and James J. Dillon."

"I don't understand."

"They were known as the Four Horsemen in the National Wrestling Alliance, or World Championship Wrestling."

"Oh, yes. That was the other wrestling organization——"

"Exactly. I would run into them when they briefly appeared on WWE's Monday Night Raw It was shortly after Ric's famous retirement ceremony."

All of a sudden, he would flashback on that night when Triple H called the entire WWE roster and the crowd to chant in unison, "Thank you, Ric."

With everyone present and accounted for, the man in the theater said. "Good day, all. I hope you had a wonderful flight. My name is Lance Steiner, a permanent employee here. We'll start out with our video presentation, and then I will explain a little bit more."

The room went dark, and then the screen came on.

"Trifecta Technologies presents our latest war simulator, Battle Plans. Gamers get to participate in a game of wits and wills against an enemy. Go through boot camp, learn the latest technological weapons, and engage in battle. This game is not for the faint of heart. "

As the presentation kept on going, more graphic scenes from the game showed up, with a final climax of a bombing exploding.

"Battle Plans.... will you survive?"

The lights came on and Steiner continued. "You will all be a part of history. As you know, war is not a pretty thing, and all the world leaders, including the British Prime Minister and the President of the United States, are fools. They send off millions and millions of your soldiers to fight, and for what?

"Soldiers fight for their country and yet they get blamed for fighting to serve oil and chemical companies. Well, enough is enough. Let all the world leaders play our game and then when they all die, we can take over. This is the war to end all wars!!"

Suddenly there's a cheer from the audience, particularly the younger generation. This really was puzzling to Kendall and Jane. "Poor guys, misguided by a maniac—-"

"Well, that would explain Bradford's attitude."

"It sure does."

The crowd would follow Steiner through the hallways, where there were displays of scale model war machines like in his mansion.

At the center of the hallways was a replica of an A-10 Warthog. The crowd would surround the replica, and out of it came Lieutenant Bradford.

"People, you are indeed welcome to be a part of the solution to end all wars. No more dealing with the Hamas, Taliban, al-queida, Somalis, Russians and Chinese. We will be the new government and we will save the world."

Another cheer came from the crowd, while Kendall and Jane remained silent.

"I am so proud to have you be a part of Trifecta Technologies, which will not only revolutionize video war games, but will revolutionize the world!!"

The crowd cheered again, except for Kendall and Jane.

More big doors opened, and there was the main computer system controlling the other computers in the place. There were empty seats in the computer desks, but somehow Kendall and Jane figured out what they will be for.

"Well" Jane replied, "that is where they plan to strap all the kidnapped world leaders and force them to play BATTLE PLANS."

"Yeah, that's what I figured. Now we need to figure out where they are keeping them."

A few moments later, General Voss, driving what looks to be a golf cart, would arrive. Bradford would stand at attention, as did the other soldiers who were around the place.

"At ease, men."

After a pause, he would smile at the crowd and say, "I'm so happy you decided to come and join Trifecta Technologies. It's been a dream of mine to use our technological advances to save the world from the tyranny of communism, the wickedness of the terrorists, and the lies of a so-called democracy. We shall have the power to rule this world, and nothing shall stop us."

More applause from the crowd save Kendall and Jane.

"Now, you should have your room keys for your living quarters, and then in a few days you'll be put to work. You may be dismissed to your assigned quarters."

Kendall and Jane would check their pockets, and sure enough there were the room keys. "It's a good thing we stole their uniforms", Jane said as she was relieved.

"Yeah. Well, we'd better get some rest."

It's as exactly what the rest of the crowd did. Most of them who just lay down, some took advantage of the cable network showing their favorite movies, and those who shared a room quickly put up a "Do Not Disturb" sign in front of their door.

While Jane would rest on her bed, Kendall took advantage of the TV, being able to watch the NFL game in which he had his big day. When he switched to another channel, it was footage of current WWE wrestlers LA Knight and AJ Styles. That was followed by old footage in which he as Colonel Cobra faced off against Brock Lesner.

That match ended up in a double disqualification after a near 15-minute battle. The fans enjoyed it because it involved two "heels".

.

Kendall would smile, as that bout with Lesner was his greatest match.

Meanwhile Jane would get up and decided to take a shower. After that, she would sit in front of the mirror to make herself pretty.

Inside the headquarters of Trifecta Technologies, General Voss would meet with Bradford and Holmes. " Gentlemen, this is indeed a historic moment. We've got many of the world leaders abducted. It's a shame that no one was able to abduct President Reynolds."

"His security was tougher to fool compared to the middle eastern ones. Their security was easy to fool", explained Holmes.

"But no matter:, said Bradford, with a smirk on his face. "He and the Prime Minister can witness history from their UN Security Council Building. We shall triumph. "

"Perhaps you're thinking that the stubborn leaders won't give in.. Personally, I think it would be great to see if the Prime Minister and President will give in and let us take over. But that would've ruin the fun out of testing their emotions."

The three of them laughed as they went out of the office and began to inspect the machinery.

:"Lieutenant, I trust you have tested each devices to make sure they are in working order."Voss would say as smiled watching the technicians monitoring them.

"General, rest assured that everything is in perfect order. Soon they will be gathered in the war room, and then the fun will begin."

"Excellent, Lieutenant. I look forward to watching the show."

A few minutes later, there was a knock on the door. "Come in", the General ordered.

In walked Madame Trembley, wearing a see-through outfit, and nothing more. "General, I have news for you."

"What is it, Madame Trembley?"

"It appears that we have two impostors in our midst."

"What ae you talking about?"

"I got a call from two people who clain to work for us, telling me they were knocked unconscious."

"Really?"

Lieutenant Bradford suddenly had a smirk on his face. "It appears that this American ex-wrestler and his French companion have infiltrated our headquarters."

Now the General started to smile. "You may be right, Lieutenant. Now the question is how do we dispose of them before they wreck our plans."

"I believe I can take care of that", Madame Trembley would say as she seductively ran her hands all over her body.

Bradford turned to the General, saying, "You know, sir, she has a really good point, and a body to match.."

With that, Madame Trembley would walk out of the business waiting room. Naturally she got a lot of looks from the other people.

She would find the quarters occupied by Kendall, so she naturally knocked on the door. As Kendall opened the door, he was quite shocked.

"What are you gonna do, tempt me out of my mind?"

"Come on, mon ami. I need to talk to you."

"Really? What about? Betraying Jane and me to your bosses??"

"I didn't know you and Jane were here, until I got a call from the two persons you knocked out and replaced."

"Okay, you know we're here. Did you plan to take us to your leader?"

Madame Trembley would not speak for a few seconds as she wiped the tears off her eyes. Finally she waled towards Kendall and asked, "Suppose I do turn you to my superiors? What will you do then?"

Kendall would suddenly smile, as Madame Trembley is unaware that Jane is behind her. "I think that you might've fallen for the oldest trick in the book."

"What are you talking about?'

Kendall wouldn't answer, but he shook his head and smiled.

By the time she could try anything, she was whacked in the face by Jane. The two really put up a good cat fight, but after the smoked cleared, Madame Trembley was left a bloody mess on her face. Kendall looked at her and said, ":Now I know what a jigsaw puzzle with a couple of pieces lost looks like..."

They drag her in and then they tend to her cuts and bruises. Kendall had lots on antiseptic wipes and so he used all to clean her up.

The two women began a shouting match in French. Finally, someone came over to break it up. It was Sergeant Holmes. He held Madame Trembley while Kendall subdued Jane.

"Well, I must say, Mr. Jacobson. You and your friend, Ms. Dow, ought to be complimented for your determination to try and stop Trifecta Technologies.You're wasting your time."

"Oh, I don't know about that,Holmes. I have nothing better to do so we decided we're gonna defeat your organization and free all the world leaders you've abducted."

Holmes would laugh maniacally. "Really? You two against us? Impossible. Trifecta Technologies is powerful enough to destroy anyone and anything that gets in our way."

Kendall would laugh after that, mocking Holmes. "You're a dumb ass if you think we didn't come prepared. Did you really think that it's just two of us who will destroy Trifecta? "

"You're bluffing!!"

"For real? You think that we're bluffing? You're even dumber that I thought."

By this time Holmes was irritated. "Enough of your games, Mr. Jacobson." He would wave his arms and shout "GUARDS!"

Three men in security uniform showed up. Holmes ordered them, "Take them to see General Voss."

Kendall would just smiled and sarcastically reply, "Oh, Goody. A field trip!!"

With that, Kendall and Jane were escorted around the building. They would pass by the Internet servers connected to one large main computer in a room, which someone is monitoring at the moment.

Holmes would go in for a brief moment, saying to the operator, "I hope everything is in working order."

"Yes, sir", replied the operator. "We'll be able to have our world leaders play BATTLE PLANS for real."

"Good", he said as he tapped him on the shoulder.

As they kept going, they entered a very spacious area, which looked like a tropical paradise. Everyone there were wearing swimsuits and having a good time.

Jane wasn't impressed. "I would rather be soaking up sun in Paris."

Kendall looked at them and shook his head. "What's this? A reward for being loyal to Trifecta?"

Holmes laughed in a triumphant matter. "You're getting smarter, Mr. Jacobson. But there is more for you to see."

They kept on going until they reached an elevator, leading to the top headquarters of Trifecta Technologies. As they go into a room filled with war dioramas and replicas of soldier uniforms, they would reach the end of the room. There were the jail cells, and int them were the abducted world leaders.

"Gentlemen, I introduce you to Mr. Kendall Jacobson, and his lovely assistant, Madame Jane Dow. These are supposed to be the ones to rescue you from us. Ha Ha. As you can tell, they have failed. SO you will be participating in BATTLE PLANS, the war to end all wars, and then Trifecta Technologies will take over."

Kendall was able to get a word in. "This guys a comedian. We'll prove that when we spring you all."

"SILENCE!!" shouted Holmes. "Now, I will bring you to General Voss."

Sure enough, they would reach the last room which had walls full of scenes from the war game, as well as scale replicas of armor vehicles and planes.

There sitting in his corner desk was General Voss, with Lieutenant Bradford standing next to him.

Holmes saluted and said, "Sir, these are the two persons who claim they will defeat us."

Obviously, Voss and Bradford saluted back.

"Well, Herr Jacobson, I finally get to meet you and Frau Dow. You two against Trifecta Technologies? HA!! Do you really think you stand a chance?"

Kendall was not intimidated as he replied, "Herr General, what makes you think you can win?"

"What makes you think you can win, Herr Jacobson?"

"Do you really think we've come alone, Herr General.? We have backup,so you boys can put your stupid idea of world domination where the sun don't shine. . HA. Tears for Fears was right."

"What?" Voss looked puzzled.

That's when Lieutenant Bradford would pull out an MP3 player, to play the Tears For Fears song "Everybody Wants To Rule The World".

"All right, Lieutenant. I've heard enough", Voss would say in disgust.

Kendall, meanwhile, would smile, saying. "I'd say that's a real catchy tune."

"You have a keen sense of humor, Herr Jacobson. But do you really think that you can stop Trifecta Technologies from taking over?"

"Try us, Herr General. You'll see."

Voss was unimpressed, and then the turned to Sergeant Holmes. ":Were they searched before you brought them here?"

"Yes, sir. Nothing but acetaminophen tablets and golf balls."

"Acetaminophen tablets and golf balls?"

Kendall would smile again. "I get headaches every time I hit over par."

Lieutenant Bradford looked impatient as he said, "General, we have wasted enough time with Jacobson and Dow. It's time we lock them up."

Voss would agree. "Sergeant, take Herr Jacobson and Fraulein Dow to their prison cell."

"Yes, sir. Right away, Herr General." agreed Holmes.

They would walk a few more steps away, and then they were led into a cell, with two separate room. Kendall was put into one, and Jane the other. Their rooms would have a bathroom, a bed and a TV set with whatever they wanted to watch. There was also a video camera, and then they would find a listening device beneath their beds.

Also next to their beds were intercoms, with a note indicating that the General will be speaking to them from time to time. It began to beep twice, and then the General's voice was heard. "Herr Jacobson—-"

"Yo, What's up?"

"Ha. Your American style of salutations are quite improper, Herr Jacobson".

"Your accommodations are atrocious. Then again, I wasn't expecting the Ramada Inn."

The General would laugh manically. "Fraulein Dow, are you comfortable?"

Jane would speak up, "I've seen better rooms in a Motel Six".

Again, the General laughed manically. "You too will need some rest. The demonstration of BATTLE PLANS will begin tomorrow at 8 PM Philippines time. You will get to see all the world leaders kill each other, just like you and your French student friends did to the terrorists in my mansion."

"This is maddening", Jane would yell. "You have no right to take away any country's government. Capitalism and socialism have been around for years. You can't have your own dictatorial form of government."

"Pity that I will have to kill you, Fraulein. It would be nice to have you around, just like.Madame Trembley.

"Oh, Madame Trembley? How do you intend to tell Lieutenant Bradford , or are you going to tell Bradford?"

"What difference does it make? Why does he have to know? The important thing is they work for me, and I care less about anything else. "

"Herr General, as the Americans would say, You Suck!!"

"Amen to that", agreed Kendall.

"That is of no importance to me", Voss said. "I only care about telling the Russians that communism is dead, socialism is phony, and democracy is failing. "

"You need a psychiatrist, Herr Voss. You've got some serious issues."

"I'm not amused by your humor, Herr Jacobson. What makes you think you defeat Trifecta Technologies?"

"You don't know me very well, do you?"

After that, it was dead silence. Jane was surprised as she said, "I never thought you would be able to shut Voss up."

"Hey, I used to do a lot of trash-talking when I was in the NFL and WWE."

"Trash-talking? "

"Sure, it a way to get to an opponent's head, through insults and telling him you're better than he is."

"We are both better than he is.":

"That's right."

At the head office, Voss had been listening tho their conversation. "This Herr Jacobson thinks he is so clever.

"Sir, I would not underestimate him", warned Sergeant Holmes. "For a former NFL player and WWE star, he's not only resilient but dangerous."

"Well, the only way to find out is tomorrow. Fraulein Trembly——"

Madame Trembley would come in the room, this time wearing a green halter top and bike shorts. "Herr General——"

"It will be your time to try to earn their trust again. I warn you, Fraulein, that if you fail, you will suffer the consequences."

"I will not fail you, Herr General."

"That's what I want to hear, Fraulein. Carry on."

With that, she walked out of the office.

Holmes was a little skeptical. "Sir, with all due respect, I don't know if we can fully trust her."

Voss would have a smirk on his face. "You have a point, Sergeant, but just like you, I don't take chances either. If we're wrong to trust her, you can kill her."

"Understood, Herr General".

"In the meantime, we just wait."

Meanwhile, Madame Trembley goes to the cells and then she talks to one of the guards. "I would like to interrogate the two prisoners. I think I can persuade them."

"You can interrogate me anytime", said the first guard.

"Make room for me", replied the second.

"Hey, I have seniority over you two", shouted the third.

"Gentlemen, the General would not like it if you start fighting over me when you should be doing your jobs.", she would say in a very seductive tone of voice.

They all smiled as they let her in. This naturally got the curiosity of Kendall and Jane, as they watched what was going on.

Once Madame Trembley faced them, Kendall would say, "What'cha trying to do? Seduce me into surrendering or something?"

"Kendall", she would speak with s smirk on her face. "I have to admit, for a former football player and former wrestler, you're very handsome." "Mom

"Yeah, mom always told me that. It's a good thing you're not my mother."

"Oh, well, I would like to know you better. You are so good with your moves—-"

By this time Jane was angry. "You little bitch. I should've finished you off a long time ago."

Jane would look at has she watched Madame Trembley open the prison door. As soon as she stepped inside, she was met with a right hood to her face.

Once this happened, it was on, as the two women would fight outside the prison. The three guards did nothing but be spectators, and even Kendall would watch in awe.

It was quite interesting watching the ladies fight. Kendall thought to himself "This is reminiscent

of the Divas matches."

Kendall proved to be very observant, for at that very moment, Madame Trembley threw a pair of nunchucks his way. He knew exactly what to do once he got them.

Just as the guards weren't looking—preoccupied with the fight going on between Jane and Madame Trembley— Kendall attacked one of them, and the ladies laid out some martial arts moves against the other two.

Once those guards became unconscious, all they had to do was to take away their weapons and ammo. Kendall decided to keep the nunchucks. "I've always wanted to use these for real."

Chapter Thirteen

Outside of the island was quite a scene as there were helicopters flying around the area. In one of the copters were Pete Snyder and Jim Underwood. The others were a team of soldiers from the country of Sudari, an Arab nation with pro-western ideals, all wearing camouflaged scuba gear.

"Okay, men, listen up", Pete would say. "We know the Trifecta Technologies' headquarters are beneath this island. We are going to go inside to rescue all the world leaders, including your Prime Minister. If you have to kill any of the Trifecta people, do it. Let's move—-"

Naturally, all the soldiers would dive into the ocean, ready to complete the task.

It was time for Jim to call Kendall on his transmitter. "ASIO to Cobra, ASIO to Cobra, come in—-"

Kendall would receive the message, "Cobra—-"

"The Cavalry is on it way. Repeat, the Cavalry is on it way."

"Copy that, ASIO. Out—-: "

With that, Jane and Madame Trembly would free the abducted world leaders while Kendall took out the cameras monitoring the area.

The signal normally monitoring the cell area was put out of commission, One of the Trifecta operators would shot, "Sir, danger at the cell block. Repeat, danger at the cell block".

General Voss, Lieutenant Bradford and Sergeant Holmes looked at the screen in horror.

"Damn that Jacobson!!"shouted Voss. "Find them, do you hear me? FIND THEM!!"

Holmes would go on the intercom. "FULL ALERT!! Saboteurs in the facility. Repeat Saboteurs in the facility!! Kill them!!"

Trifecta's soldiers come out and then attempt to join in the party.

Down at the area leading to the prison, some of the guards were able to make it to the basement. It was as far as they could go as the security door was locked and inoperative.

"General, we can't get into the prison entrance. The security door is jammed. \"

By this time the General was furious. "Wait there. I'll get you out somehow."

He would open the control box that lead to the buttons to open any security door.

\

Meanwhile, the rebel soldiers arrived from the sub bay area. The world leaders were all present and accounted for.

Just then a submarine came out of the water. In it were British sailors, sent out to rescue them. "Come on in and hurry!!" shouted the voice inside the sub. The rebels would help them get in.

Kendall showed up just to see the sub leave, so he spoke to the rebel soldiers with them. "Okay, it's time to put Trifecta Technologies out of business."

"We are with you all the way", said the leader of the rebel soldiers.

The alarm would sound, and the battle would begin. It felt as if BATTLE PLANS was being played for real without the computer and software.

As the battle raged on, the three heroes would make their way to the main computer. It was time for them to destroy the hardware, including the IT equipment.

A few minutes later, Holmes would arrive."Jacobson, you're a dead man."

Just then two other Trifecta workers showed up, and it was a battle of fisticuffs as Kendall would fight Holmes while the ladies fought against the two Trifecta loyalists. Kendall used the nunchucks with great expertise, while the ladies' martial arts proved too much for their rivals.

The fight between Kendall and Holmes would last a little longer because Holmes was able to use a chair to counter-act against the nunchucks. That's when Jane would use her little rock and managed to hit Holmes in the middle of his head. That made him throw the chair at Jane, but he missed.

Kendall wouldn't as he was able to do a thrust kick on him, forcing him to land on shrapnel from a broken table placed upside down at the time.

"Well, I got my point across", he said after Jane and Madame Trembley finished off their foes.

Jane would smile. "Well, as you Americans would say, 'It's time to kick butt."

Kendall would smile back and say, "Or to apply some Austin 3:16…"

Without hesitation, they would join in on the gun battle against the Trifecta armed forces, but they knew their main goal was to find Lieutenant Bradford and General Voss.

Speaking of those two, they were still in the office monitoring the situation through their large screen.

Voss started to throw a few insignificant objects around the room, shouting "KILL JACOBSON!!"

At this time Bradford was unable to control him. "Sir, it's time we get out of he, right now!"

Voss gave an evil stare at Bradford and said, "This is what I get for trusting your daughter!!"

Bradford was confused. "My what? Sir, what are you talking about?"

"I'll tell you what I'm talking about!! Fraulein Trembley is your estranged daughter!!"

"No! No, sir. You're being delusional—-"

"I am not, Herr Loitman. I found out who she was by investigating her background, her DNA,and fingerprints. There's no doubt about it. Trembly is your daughter"

"Why, you——-"

A struggle happened between the two villains, and during the struggle apparently the General pressed a red button, which started an air-raid like sound, followed by a voice sound saying, "Attention. Danger Point active in two hours; Evacuate immediately."

"Bradford began to panic."You filthy sonofa——"

Punches were thrown between the two of them, while Kendall, Jane, and Madame Trembley finally made it to the room after a heated battle against Voss' associates.

Madame Trembley suddenly yelled, "Papa!!"

Bradford managed to knock out Voss, and then he turned to her. "Margot? Is it true?"

"Yes. I fooled Trifecta Technologies to become his personal assistant, but I was trying to save you from him. He killed Pierre Francios, whose real last name is Pierre Trembley.."

"And you're his——"

"Granddaughter."

Suddenly the voice warning system sounded, "Evacuate immediately. You have one hour and 45 minutes."

Kendall would say, ":Look, we've got to get out of here right now."

They would start running out of the office, unaware that General Voss regained consciousness. He would get his gun at was about to kill Bradford when Kendall saw it and shouted, "LOOK OUT!!"

Fortunately it missed. They would keep running with General Voss hot on their tail.

Reaching the runway, they would find the jetliner. Bradford would turn the switch on to activate the dome and raise the runway to the island level, while Kendall would get the jet ready for takeoff.

By the time it reached the island level and the dome was removed, Bradford was ready to board the plane, but not before seeing Voss go on one of the attack helicopters.

As Bradford would give Margot a hug, he would say, "Jacobson, Voss is taking one of the attack helicopters!!"

"We'll get out of this safely," Kendall acknowledged.

The jet plane would make it up, but the helicopter was close behind.

"Once we get back to the states, Lieutenant, you'll get to talk tp to the secretary of defense.

"All right. SO I can get these golf balls ready for Genreal Voss. Can you take over the plane?"

"Yes, I can."

With that, Bradford and Margot would go to the cockpit and take over, while Kendall would prepare one of the exploding golf balls, some chewing gum and the projectile. Naturally he would chew the gum.

Gunfire came from the helicopter. Voss would laugh manically as he shot those machine guns out. The good news is that it didn't manage to do any damage to the jetliner.

Kendall had it in his sights. He had open one of the doors of the plane to make sure he has a clear shot at it.,

Minutes later, he sees the attack helicopter in his sights. Waiting until it got closer, his fires the golf ball right at the unsuspecting Voss.

BOOM!!! General Voss is history.

Kendall's celebratory victory was a memorable one. Jane was jumping for joy, and Bradford and his daughter were also celebrating.

After he closed the door, he exhaled and said. "That's my best hole-in-one."

Jane would start laughing, "Is that what they call, 'par for the course'"?

Epilogue

The location was the Toyota Center in Houston, in front of a sold-out crowd. Among those in attendance were the US Marines and members of the NFL Houston Texans.

The pyrotechnics went underway as WWE Champion Cody Rhodes made an appearance in front of a cheering crowd.

Once the crowd quieted down a bit, Cody would welcome everyone to the Toyota Center. After the cheer, he would continue:

"You know, we have a lot of heroes in attendance here tonight. First, we got members of our United States Marines over here."

The crowd would cheer again and the US Marines would all take a bow.

"Yes", Cody continued, "thank you all for your service. We appreciate it very much.

"Now, it's time to congratulate and thank another hero. Recently, some of our world leaders were abducted by a madman and his goofy henchmen. So who did the government send to rescue those leaders and lay some whoop-ass against this whacko??

"Well, we used to hate this guy, but now we cheer him for saving our country from an evil madman. Let's give it up for the man we used to know as Colonel Cobra, Kendall Jacobson!!!:

As the crowd cheered and gave a standing ovation, Kendall would out of the ramp entrance, along with Jane Dow, both were smiling.

"You know, Kendall, America is proud of what you did, and for that we salute you!!"

The crowd cheered loudly and the Marines sitting in front would stand up and applaud. Moved by the reception, he would smile and do a thank you wave.

Finally, members of the Houston Texans would lead a chant of "Cobra!! Cobra!!" Kendall would smile again, and he'd get a big hug from Jane.

He had his fame in college football, the NFL, the WWE, and now as an ASIO Super Spy.

The End